catch me

BOOK ONE OF THE REBEL COURT

BOOKS BY ALIANNE DONNELLY

BLOOD AND SHADOWS
Blood Moons
Blood Trails
Blood Debts
Blood Hunt

DAWN OF RAGNAROK
The Royal Wizard
Dragonblood
Prince of Deceit

THE BEAST
Bastien
The Beast

OTHER TITLES
Wolfen
Virtual
Function: L1VE

catch me

ALIANNE DONNELLY

THIS IS AN ALIANNE DONNELLY BOOK PUBLISHED BY ALIANNE DONNELLY
It's not bragging if it's true.

CATCH ME is a work of fiction. Names, characters, places, and incidents either are the product of the author's imagination or are used fictitiously, and any resemblance to actual persons, living or dead, business establishments, events, or locales is entirely coincidental.

aliannedonnelly.com

ISBN: 978-1-948325-32-5

Published in the United States of America

Rebel heroes deserve rebel dedications. With that in mind…

*This story is dedicated with love to those who said I couldn't do this.
For giving me the great pleasure of proving you wrong.*

CHAPTER 1

Bloody fucking hell, I thought we were done with this shite when she took the throne."

"As eloquent as ever, Graeme," Haig drawled, his gaze following the sway of a truly exemplary female ass down the opulent corridor. As if she felt his gaze, the woman's shoulders stiffened, and she paused to look over her shoulder. Haig gave her his most winning grin and a bold once-over, delighted when she blushed and rushed off around the corner. He craned his neck to prolong the sight, but damn, she was quick!

There was a distinct note of an eye roll in Graeme's voice when he muttered, "And you're still a whore."

Beau sighed. "Haig, leave Miss Juliana alone."

Haig raised an eyebrow at his comrade. Of all of them, Beau was the only one who'd weathered the war without apparent injury. To be expected, given he'd never actually seen any of the battles he'd strategized. Foot soldiers met the enemy in the field. Men like Beau conducted them like a well-trained orchestra from behind the scene. "Miss Juliana, is it? You saving her for yourself? You dirty dog, you."

The glare Beau spared him would have been truly frightening, if not for the blush coloring his pale cheeks. "You know full well the royal staff is off limits."

"Or are you saving yourself for her?" Haig winked. "That it?" When the rest of the rebels joined Beau in the glaring contest, Haig decided to be merciful. "You're all just jealous that I get more pussy in a day than you did in all of last year."

"Sebastian's got you beat," Beau returned. "*Handily.*"

Haig scowled at that. It wasn't a competition! "Where is he, any-way?"

"In treatment," Declan said in a tone that signaled the discussion was over. Haig had long ago stopped being intimidated by the Ra-venskin's piercing silver gaze, but when Declan glowered like that, even the strongest resolve to win the staring contest failed miserably. At an imposing six feet five inches, and with his skin as black as a raven's feather—hence the name—he was intimidating as hell at the best of times.

Haig held up his hands in mock surrender.

Graeme growled, tugging on the collar of his dress shirt. "How much bloody longer will she make us wait?" He shoved to his feet to pace the hallway, checking his watch every five seconds. "This is bullshite. The summons said noon sharp."

"Yeah, and that's still five minutes away." Haig couldn't help star-ing at the man in horrified wonder. Graeme took issue with fancy clothes. Even their tasteful uniforms, made to size and specially for them, seemed to make his shaggy hair stand on end. Haig had been told Graeme used to be something to look at back in the day. He couldn't see it. To him, Graeme was and forever would be a rude, werewolf-looking guy who was allergic to razor blades, chewed his nails off when they got too long, and bit people who tried to cut his hair.

Animal...

Darius, having observed the exchange quietly until now, frowned in thought. "What do you think this is about? Beau, did she say any-thing to you?"

Beau raised an eyebrow. "Did the queen of Valefort tell me why she was summoning the leaders of her uprising all at once on short notice? No. It never came up."

Haig snorted. "What did?"

Darius ignored him. "You're her right hand. Surely you know something."

Beau shrugged uncomfortably. "Nothing concrete. Just whispers. The Network's been buzzing and the castle's been upside down ever since Snow White took the crown. Could be anything."

"Gentlemen, gentlemen," Haig quickly interjected. Darius was like a tick. Once he latched on to a mystery, he didn't let go until he was fully satisfied. "Why waste the energy wondering? In two minutes, we'll be called in and find out exactly what's what. Take a page out of Saxon's book. He couldn't care less."

Judging from his slouch and the tilt of his head, Saxon not only didn't care, he was fast asleep. Again. *How the hell does he do that?*

The grandfather clock at the end of the corridor struck noon and the grand door opened. As if on cue, at precisely the same moment, Sebastian rounded the corner and jogged up to the rest of them, still buttoning his shirt. Haig shook his head, reminding himself, *It's not a contest.*

Snow White's herald, a proud, but ancient, withered little man did his best to fill the doorway while they all stood up. Saxon had to be shoved awake, but to his credit, he recovered quickly. The herald looked down his beaked nose at them for a moment, then inclined his head a fraction of an inch as if he'd judged them acceptable— barely. "Her Majesty thanks you for your audience." All of them started forward to enter, but the herald stayed them. "One at a time, if you please. Her Majesty will see Master Haig first."

They shared a look amongst them. This was new.

Haig grinned wide at his comrades. "I'll try not to wear her out too much."

They rolled their eyes at him, so he flipped them off and followed the herald.

Since Snow White's ascension, Valefort wasn't so much a kingdom as it was a thriving corporation with Snow as the CEO, and her receiving room reflected that. Queen Zorana's garishly appointed, cavernous throne room had been stripped of all gild and trimmings. The golden tapestries had been replaced with TV monitors showing the latest economic trends and forecasts, the dais had been demolished, and a massive circle of high-gloss ebony tables took up the middle, surrounded by cushy power chairs.

Snow White—Queen Snow now—stood at the far side of the table, dressed in a stylish business suit, her raven hair woven into a single braid over one shoulder. She smiled in welcome. "Haig. It's been too long."

Haig grinned and shocked a gasp out of the herald when he rounded the tables in ground-eating strides and hugged the queen off her feet.

Snow was still laughing when he set her back on them. "Marlow, that'll be all for now. Thank you."

The herald bowed away and closed the door behind him.

"It's good to see you again, brat," Haig said, tugging on her braid. "Where's that no good husband of yours?"

"Marcus won't be joining us today," she replied easily enough, but something in her tone put Haig on guard. Reading his expression with her signature know-it-all-ness, Snow gasped. "Oh, no! There's nothing wrong between us. We're blissfully happy. Really. It's just that… I don't want to involve him in this. It's something of a delicate matter."

A delicate matter she couldn't share with the rest of her allies—men who'd saved her life, sheltered her, protected her, and led her to victory against the murderous Queen Zorana. Men she'd lovingly dubbed her Rebel Court, once upon a time. Haig's ever-present good humor faded. "Then we'd better get down to business."

She allowed him to seat her, then motioned for him to take the adjacent chair. "What I'm about to tell you cannot leave this room. You can't tell anyone, not even the other six, and Marcus must never find out. If he did, he'd turn it into a witch hunt, and that's the last thing I need right now."

"You want someone disappeared." It was a logical conclusion.

"Yes. I'm afraid I do."

Good humor definitely gone. This had to be serious. Snow only had to speak a word and any enemy, political or otherwise, could be dispatched by an expert marksman or a spell. She wouldn't have called him in for something as easy as an assassination. His presence here meant that whoever had drawn Snow's wrath needed to be erased quietly and completely. "Who's the mark?"

She took a deep breath. "Zorana's son."

Haig frowned. "Zorana had a son?"

"Believe me, I was as surprised as you are," she retorted. "Although, I really shouldn't have been, given what we know about her."

His mind refused to wrap all the way around that. "You may need to back up a little here. What exactly do we know and how did we find out?"

Snow gave him a half-hearted smile. "Funny things you come across when you go through your traitor stepmother's things. Among the *many* ledgers of illegal magic dealings, I found bundles of personal diaries."

"So now you know all of Zorana's sordid secrets?"

"Emphasis on sordid." Her expression turned pained, hands twisting in her lap. Given that Zorana had hated Snow enough to want her dead in a way most foul, whatever she may have written into her diaries couldn't have been pleasant for Snow to read.

Haig caught her hand in his, squeezed lightly. "Take your time."

Snow shook off her gloom and smiled. "Anyway, yes. Apparently, Zorana had a son several months after she married my father. It's all just obscure enough that there's no way to tell whether the issue was legitimate."

"You know he's not."

"Do I?"

"Will it make a difference, anyway?"

Snow shook her head in the negative. "By the word of our Charter, any child born after the wedding takes place is considered true and legitimate, and the crown legally belongs to the first-born *son*, only to pass to a daughter if no male heir exists at the time of the monarch's death."

"Which means this boy could challenge your rule, and by the word of our Charter, you'd have to abdicate to him or risk another civil war."

"And there would definitely be a war. We may have won against

Zorana's armies, but she still has too many sympathizers among the noble court. People who have lost a lot in terms of wealth and standing when she was executed. It wouldn't take much to incite them against me."

"So we take care of the problem," Haig offered with a shrug. "Easy enough. Where is he?"

Snow winced. "That's kind of the problem."

Haig glowered. "I'm not going to like this, am I?"

"From what I could decipher, Zorana hid the boy somewhere in the Elderwood."

"Aw, fuck." While the castle city of Kesteran and most towns of a certain size were modernized with electricity, indoor plumbing, heat, and refined magic, a large portion of the land was still mired in the Dark Ages of brow sweat and raw magic only. People in the Elderwood lived in hovels and hauled water from the creek—if one happened to be nearby. And the worst part was, because of the effects raw magic had on the environment, no modern technology worked there. No phones, tracking devices, combustion engines, even weapons. "How am I supposed to find him?"

"You'll be working with—"

"Absolutely not!"

"—a partner for this assignment," she finished, ignoring his outburst. "I know you don't want anyone knowing about your…skills. I swore to you I would never tell anyone, and I haven't—I won't. But you can't find a needle of a teenage boy in a haystack the size of the Elderwood on your own."

"Oh, and I can just imagine the natural wonder you chose to help me track him."

"Aislin Crane," she answered regally.

Haig gaped at her. "The Huntsman's daughter?"

"She's the best tracker in Valefort." And considering Zorana had her father quartered for allowing Snow to escape, Haig could see how Aislin might be motivated to strike back at the bitch. "But I don't want her to know who the mark is."

"What? Why?"

She gave him a look. "Because she might balk if she finds out the boy you're about to take out is only fifteen years old."

"Well how the hell is she going to track him if she doesn't know who he is?"

Snow shrugged. "You have your gifts, she has hers."

"Fan-*fucking*-tastic."

Snow's face shuttered, and she drew herself up. "Will you do this or not?"

He scoffed. "Do I get a choice?"

She gave him a sweet smile and pressed a button on her desk to open an automatic door.

Grumbling under his breath, Haig pushed to his feet and squared his shoulders in preparation to meet his new partner.

CHAPTER 2

Your Majesty," the woman said right by Haig's shoulder.

"*Gah!* Don't you make noise?" The last word drew out of him as he turned to face her.

Aislin was tall, just a couple of inches shorter than him, dressed in soft, clinging leathers that hugged her curves in all the right places. They were sewn together from odd-colored pieces, in a pattern that invited the eye to follow a meandering path from her exposed collarbones, down the valley of her pillowy cleavage, across her flat stomach to just past her loins.

That's where Haig stuck, hissing a breath. *Mercy...* She had nicely rounded hips, ripe for gripping, and long, supple legs that would easily lock around him as he thrust into her. Gods, he loved long-legged women. He loved all women, but there was something special about the leggy ones. An elegance and a sensuality usually reserved for swans and does.

"That would be counterproductive for a hunter," she retorted, drawing his attention—slowly—back up to her face. She'd braided her thick, black hair tightly against her scalp, throwing her features into stark relief. Haughtily arched eyebrows, cold, piercing green eyes, a narrow, aristocratic nose, high cheekbones...she had all the makings of an ice queen. But her soft skin was the color of warm, creamy caramel and her mouth was plump and generous, the lower lip thicker than the upper, hinting at rich reserves of passion he'd love to mine. The things he could do to that mouth alone…

Suddenly the boardroom was gone, and Haig's magic hijacked his mind, thrusting him into another place, another time, into another version of him in some alternate reality where…

The Huntsman's daughter stood naked at the edge of a lake, her face turned up to the light of a bright, full moon. She smiled at him with a challenge in her eyes as she backed into the water until the surface waves lapped at the juncture of her thighs.

She shivered, her dark nipples beading instantly, and Haig almost went to his knees. The sight of her like this—wild, unabashed, utterly beautiful—caused an ache in his chest. He wanted to stare at her for hours, and at the same time, he wanted desperately to be in that lake with her—inside her. Somehow, he came forward, joined her in the water, fully dressed, his pants straining across a raging cockstand. For her and no one else.

The random thought should have scared the shit out of him, but when Aislin lay back, floating weightless on the water, with moonlight burnishing her soft skin in cool, silver hues like a magical gift laid out just for him, Haig no longer cared…

Snow cleared her throat, dragging him out of the vision and back to the present. "Haig Cavanaugh, I'd like to introduce Aislin Crane." Under her breath she added, "You're staring."

Of course he was staring! She'd just introduced him to sex on a stick, whom he was apparently sexing up right now in at least one other reality. How was he supposed to get anything done, know-ing that—*seeing* it? "Hi," he said, buying himself time to recover his power of speech. *Down!* he commanded his dick. It had no effect whatsoever.

Aislin scoffed delicately, and the room temperature plunged into arctic levels when she gave him a careless once-over. "You're sup-posed to be the expert?"

Despite her arch tone, Haig fought down a hot shiver. She had a soft, just-been-thoroughly-fucked kind of voice that shot straight to his groin. "Jack of all trades," he heard himself saying, "and master of quite a few. Care to give me a try?" Instinctively, he knew she'd be just as quiet in bed and, gods, he itched to break her of that. He knew how to do things to her that would drive her out of her head with pleasure. He could make her scream his name and weep with gratitude. And beg him for more—

Dismissing him off hand, Aislin turned to Snow, giving him a full-body view of her profile: a proud, straight line from the top of her head to the heel of her soft-soled boot, disrupted only by the curve of her breasts and ass. Her arms were bare, visibly toned, but not mannish. She'd smeared them with soot, presumably for camouflage. He noticed the crossbow she clutched in her left hand. A bolt quiver was strapped to her right thigh.

Oh, man. Haig's mouth watered just thinking about all the ways he could disarm her and strip her naked. He swayed on his feet, plunging right back into his vision. Only this time…

He stood between Aislin's thighs, and her head was tilted back, her mouth open on a passionate sigh. He saw his own hands on her; felt the heated silk of her skin, the curl of her legs around him, and he thought, It's even better than in a bed.

The folds of her sex rubbed up and down over his cock, each stroke bringing him to the very edge of her pussy, teasing with the promise of entrance.

She was magnificent, stunning, an otherworldly nymph, and he felt so…grateful. Aislin arched, crying out as an orgasm shivered through her exquisite body—but how could she deny him the sight of her face? With her legs squeezing him to her, Haig lowered to his haunches in the water, bringing her upright into his arms. Eyes unfocused, Aislin sighed his name, just as Haig thrust up, plunging straight into heaven…

"…choose your horse from the stables," Snow was saying, "and have the kitchen prepare supplies for—"

With his attention still halfway in visionland, Haig licked his suddenly dry lips, staring hard at the true Huntress standing before him. Only, in his mind, she was still naked, and very, very wet. And he still felt her sheath squeezing his cock. "What are you, a size six? Eight?" he asked, hoarse-voiced.

Snow gaped at him.

Aislin speared him with a hateful glare. "I make my own clothes."

"Yeah, I bet you do."

"From the skins of my enemies," she added with a savage smile. "I save the foreskins for polishing rags."

Haig's balls pulled up so tight he almost went soprano for a second. "And I'll bet you can't wait to get your hands on mine." This cruel streak was so unlike the sensual version of her from his vision, it jarred him fully back to the present, but his interest didn't abate at all. In fact, he almost liked this Aislin better. Haig had always loved a good challenge, and hers promised to be epic.

Then she raised an eyebrow and he realized what he'd just said. "Wait, that didn't come out right."

"What's wrong with you?" Snow hissed, blushing furiously. "You know what? Don't answer that. Just get out of my sight. Both of you."

Aislin bowed and strode to the corridor leading to the stables.

Haig watched the sway of her hips, savoring the athleticism and power encased in her sexy leathers. That one would be a ride he'd remember for the rest of his life. He knew it for a fact because, in an alternate reality somewhere, another version of him already did.

He had just enough brain power left not to adjust himself in the queen's presence. But he couldn't help grinning at her. "I'm going to enjoy this."

Snow crossed her arms. "If you do anything to make her regret taking you along, I will personally cut off your genitals and gift them to her for polishing rags."

"What is it with you two and polishing things with my junk? You can't come up with a better use for it? Seriously, I thought *you* at least would have more imagination than that."

She rubbed her brow and sighed in exasperation. "Just do the job, okay? That's all I ask."

"Oh, I'll do the job. If anyone can do the job, it's me." Haig winked. "I'll do that job *real* nice."

Fuming, she pointed to the corridor after Aislin.

With a heel-clicking salute, he loped off in pursuit of his lovely Huntress.

"Hey, wait up!"

Aislin picked up her step. The corridor split into two up ahead. With any luck, he'd take the wrong turn and end up in the dungeons.

Useless, annoying waste of a man! Never would Aislin have imagined the pragmatic queen pairing her with that…that whore! There wasn't a female in Kesteran who didn't know Haig Cavanaugh. If not personally, then by reputation. He was a wastrel, a libertine. How he'd managed to earn such high honors during the war she'd never know. His only true skill seemed to be fucking.

The only thing that kept Aislin from refusing this mission was her faith that Queen Snow *was* a pragmatic regent. Which meant she had to have a reason for pairing them together. *Just ignore the stupidity,* she told herself. *Focus on the mission. Find the target. The sooner you do that, the sooner you can put this whole embarrassment behind you.*

Footsteps pounded behind her with all the subtlety of a stampeding moose. "Hey, partner," Haig called, delivering a sound smack on her ass as he passed by. "Race you there!"

She had a bolt drawn and aimed at the back of his head in two seconds. But her hands shook too much with the force of her fury to make the shot. Her ass tingling where he'd pawed her, she removed the bolt, but clutched it like a dagger as she stalked him into the stables.

"Goran," she greeted the hostler with a respectful nod.

He tipped his hat in return. Having been appraised of the situation already, he'd brought forth two horses already saddled and burdened with gear, and she was gratified to see her favorite, a lovely brown mare by the name of Emer, was one of them. Aislin fastened her crossbow in place on the saddle hook, then checked over the mare and the saddlebags to make sure her necessities had been included.

"So," the whore murmured by her ear, and for just a second, she froze, barely stifling a shiver. How had he managed to sneak up on her? "Shall we get this sexual tension between us taken care of now or after?"

Aislin whirled around and grasped him by the throat, a bolt in her free hand, but to her utter shock, he was faster. With a laugh, he caught her bolt hand as his foot slipped around hers. With a deft twist, he knocked her off balance and her back met a stall door. Her other hand, still at his neck, went limp as he leaned into her. "Straight to the point. I like that in a woman."

"How did you do that?" She could have thrown him a dozen different ways, yet her body remained pliant. Because, somehow, he felt...familiar.

Haig's sinful blue eyes danced with mirth behind a stray lock of blond hair. Almost nose to nose with her, he leaned in closer still, his body pinning her in place from chest to hip. Just enough to feel his weight, the lean muscles of his torso, and the hard ridge of his erection. "I'll never tell," he whispered, his mouth a hair's breadth from hers.

Aislin pressed her lips together into a firm line. *Get ahold of yourself! This is Haig bloody Cavanaugh!* Bracing a foot against the wall, she tensed to shove him off her.

But before the thought could translate into action, his nose brushed hers, and then his mouth was at her ear. "I can feel the fight in you." His tongue darted out to touch her lobe. "You're all aquiver to break free." He put his nose to the sensitive skin of her neck and sucked in a deep breath. "But it's not me you're fighting." His teeth caught the small golden hoop of her earring, tugged a little, eliciting a surprised gasp. "The sooner you admit it, the better off both of us will be."

"Get—off—me," she grated, struggling to keep her breathing even.

"If looks could kill," he murmured with a satisfied smirk, "yours would scorch me to the bone." He released her, his knuckles brushing down her side, seemingly by accident.

Aislin doubted anything this man did was accidental. It was all a deliberate ploy—a look here, a touch there, all with one final goal in mind: seduction. She knew that, dammit! So why was her body still humming?

"I'll meet you at the castle gate at sunset," he called over his shoulder, heading out on foot.

Her mind was slow to catch up. "What? What do you mean? We're leaving now!" She chased him around the horses just in time to watch him stroll out into the courtyard with his hands in his pockets.

"Got stuff to do," he tossed back. "Things to pick up. Goodbyes to say. Long, languorous love to make." Turning mid-stride, he grinned while walking backwards away from her. "See? If you'd just admitted your lust for me, we could have saved *hours*."

CHAPTER 3

The Faery globes spelled to activate with waning sunlight shone brightly by the time the whore came bounding up to the castle gate, a satchel in hand and his shirt half off. Aislin wrinkled her nose in distaste. "You're late."

Instead of mounting his horse and setting off for the Elderwood, the bastard stopped just before her, tilted his head back, and inhaled deeply as if savoring the night air. He did it on purpose, to show off his ripped abs. Not that she paid any attention to them whatsoever. Or remember how he'd felt pressed into her from chest to knee. Or willed his low-slung pants to droop just a little lower.

He might have charmed his way under scores of skirts in Kesteran, but Aislin was immune to his cheap tricks!

Was his shirt *torn*? Those were definitely scratch marks on his stomach. Good gods, the man was shameless!

"My dear Ash, I've got to teach you to relax a little."

"We are not here to relax," she reminded him. "We are on a mission, for which you made me wait an entire day while you went off whoring. You're unsuitably dressed"—*undressed* was more accurate—"you're unprepared, and your presence alone insults me."

He chuckled, setting her teeth on edge. "Is that all?"

"And don't call me Ash!"

Haig clucked his tongue to summon his mount, a chestnut gelding named Romper. Vaulting into the saddle, Haig raised an eyebrow in challenge. "You're in such a hurry to get going, let's see if you can keep up. *Hya!*"

Shouting curses in the old tongue, Aislin prodded Emer to match Haig's breakneck pace until the darkened streets became a blur. Soon, they left the market square behind and she was forced to admit that Haig was an excellent horseman. Damn him. Moments later, the squat dwellings of the outer neighborhoods were gone and they rode through miles of fields and meadows.

At the Elderwood's border, Haig came to a full stop. Before them, a wall of trees stretched toward the sky. No cobblestoned walkways here, or even stomped dirt paths. No electricity or Faery globes, only the black of midnight warning that beyond this curtain lay wilderness.

Aislin felt as if she was standing on some kind of precipice. She knew the laws of the Elderwood—no one entered its depths without being altered in some inexplicable way. After so many years of hunting here she'd thought she'd have been used to it by now, but tonight the feeling was much more intense. Her bones hummed with something like Destiny, and a nervous flutter in her chest made her knees clench around Emer's sides until the mare fidgeted.

Haig struck a flint, lighting the candle in his lantern. "Let's go."

Taken aback by his sudden grim-faced determination, she allowed him to take the lead.

"Stay close," he warned. "The Elderwood is a treacherous old bitch."

"The Elderwood is my second home," she returned, but tightened her hold on Emer's reins all the same. "If you can't handle it, you should have stayed in yours." A cold breeze raised goose bumps along her bare arms. Too quiet. The forest ought to have been buzzing with night creatures.

"Oh, that's right. I forgot I was travelling with a foreskin-collecting savage." Haig's voice was tense, lacking his irreverent lilt of humor. Did he sense the same thing she did?

"There's a glen not far from here. We can camp there for the rest of the night." Water behaved in strange ways in the Elderwood, appearing and disappearing in the blink of an eye, leading travelers astray. Places where it remained static created watering holes that were considered sacred by humans as well as animals of all species. No blood could be spilled in them.

"How rustic," he said. "I suppose it's too much to ask for a traveler's inn?"

"This close to the border, you wouldn't find anything but thieves' dens and brothels."

"Excellent! Which way?"

Aislin bit back an annoyed growl. "Haven't you had enough of that for one day?"

"My dear Ash, one can *never* have enough of *that.*"

An owl hooted not far ahead.

Aislin pulled her hunting knife out of her boot sheath. "We're being watched."

"The Elderwood's eyes see all," Haig quoted. "If you hear whispers, let me know immediately."

"Why?"

"They might be forest nymphs looking for a lover."

She rolled her eyes. "Forest nymphs are a myth."

"You don't know that!"

"And even if they weren't, the legend you're referring to says they kill their lovers upon sunrise."

A pause. "I honestly can't think of a better way to die."

A soft trickle of water drew the horses off course toward the right, and moments later, they emerged in the glen. "Looks like you'll have to be satisfied with just me tonight."

"Is that an invitation?" he asked softly.

Her face heated and her breath caught. Even knowing this was all a game to him, Aislin couldn't help being affected by that voice, and those sinful blue eyes staring at her with so much intensity. Such was the nature of his power over women—she'd do well to remember that.

Aislin scoffed. "You wish."

"Most fervently," he returned without breaking eye contact, and just like that, Aislin's knees clenched hard on Emer's sides. She could easily imagine what a man like him would dream. No doubt he preferred his women in red lace lingerie, spread out on a massive bed of silk sheets. By all accounts, he was an extremely skilled lover; played a woman's body like an expert musician. Rumor said that he'd do anything to bring a woman to orgasm—or ten—and that bed play was a marathon sport for him.

Aislin swallowed with some difficulty. Dismounting to break away from his disconcerting stare, she knelt by the stream, bowed her head for a quick, silent prayer of thanks to the forest gods, then braced her hands on the edge of the bank and lowered to take a sip.

"Why do you hate me so much?" Haig asked right next to her, and she sputtered. How the bloody hell did he keep doing that? Settling on his haunches, he dipped his bottle in the creek. "I knew your father, you know. The fabled Alder Crane. Royal Huntsman and master falconer. They said his arrow could hit a squirrel clean through the eye at a hundred yards." He took a drink, then stared at the bottle in his hand. "A good man."

"He paid for it with his life," Aislin said thickly. All these years later and it still hurt to remember. Back then, she hadn't understood why her father had been so determined to stay, even knowing Queen Zorana would kill him for his treachery. He could have run away, hidden here in the Elderwood like Snow White had, and Zorana never would have found him.

Haig nodded. "Do you know what he told us when he brought Snow White to our cave? He said, 'I entrust the future into your keeping.'" A sad half-smile brought out faint laugh lines on his face. Suddenly he looked older, graver. No longer the clown and libertine, for the first time, the man sitting next to Aislin looked like a true warrior burdened by memories of death. "And there we were, outcasts and criminals, looking at this innocent young girl, and I thought, 'The man must have lost his damned mind!'"

Aislin didn't know what to say to that. It suddenly struck her that, were it not for the Rebel Seven, Valefort would be a much different place today. Silence stretched on as they both became lost in their thoughts, Haig staring at his hands, Aislin studying him. Perhaps there was some substance beneath that lecherous veneer after all. Aislin had seen the war take its toll on the people she knew and loved; their eyes were just as haunted as Haig's. Those shadows couldn't be faked, only disguised.

For a moment, she felt an involuntary kinship with Haig that somehow went deeper than shared suffering. For better or worse, they were on the same side, fighting the same battle, inside and out. They simply chose different methods. Maybe there was more to Haig than she'd first thought.

Aislin wasn't aware of moving, but the next thing she knew, her hand was on Haig's arm, and her lips pressed to his. She felt his sharp intake of breath, the way he tensed in surprise. Heat flooded her cheeks as she drew back, aware of how badly she'd misstepped and not entirely sure what had driven her to it.

Haig caught her elbow to stay her, pulled with gentle, inexorable pressure to bring her back. His mouth found hers, brushed back and forth, teased her lips apart. He nipped her gently, then licked between her lips, seeking entrance. Aislin forgot to breathe. His tongue played catch with hers, touching briefly, then retreating as if he was trying to lure her out. He teased, holding back and then delving deeper, but never as deep as she needed him. The maddening back and forth made her dizzy, and then he leaned away, forcing her to follow or break contact.

Aislin took the lure, shifted closer, straddled him so he wouldn't slip away again, and then she took her due. She kissed him with a fervor utterly alien to her level-headed nature. His taste was addictive; the feel of his arms around her, his hand spearing down the back of her pants to cup the curve of her ass…

Haig groaned, curling his fingers into her flesh, bringing her hard against him. "I knew it," he said against her lips, then rocked his hips up and kissed her again, stealing her breath before she could speak. "I knew you'd be like this. And now"—with one hand sliding deeper between her legs and the other tangled in her hair, he arched her neck to lick her pulse—"I know how to get to you."

With his fingers playing at her wet pussy, his words were slow to penetrate, but when they did, Aislin frowned. "What?" He stroked her again, the tip of his finger dipping inside just barely, but enough to make her clench. Gods, it felt so good, she almost gave into it. Almost. Clutching his hair, she yanked him away from feasting on the sensitive spot where her neck met her shoulder to force his gaze to hers.

His drunken smile made his words all the more a mockery. "Naturally, a huntress will want to hunt. All I have to do is make *you* want to chase *me*. And then let you catch me."

Her ardor cooled so quickly she shivered. Haig smiled wider, misinterpreting her reaction, and pushed that probing finger a little deeper. That little twitch of movement, aimed with such precision, as if he knew exactly where she needed it, teased with the promise of unimaginable pleasures still to be had. If Aislin didn't know better, she might have let this play out. But she did know better—she *did*, dammit! "Haig," she crooned, shifting for better balance as she oh so sensuously removed his hand from her pants.

"Hmm?" He was already pulling on the laces of her bodice, straining against her hold to get back to kissing her neck.

"You reek of brothel scum. I think you need a bath." Bracing her feet in the dirt, she threw her weight back, pulling him along. With a knee to his chest, she used their momentum against him, sending him flying over her head, straight into the creek. A shower of water droplets rained down on her. For all the warmth of summer, the creek was freezing. Cold enough to cool even the whore's ardor.

But Haig came up laughing even as he sputtered. "You play dirty, my sweet. I'll remember that." And then, to Aislin's dismay, he proceeded to give her exactly what she'd asked for. Without any hint of bashfulness, he stripped out of his sodden clothes, tore out a clump of moss and began to scrub himself, singing a jaunty tune.

With the water as clear as crystal and the light of their lanterns just bright enough, Aislin discovered that not even a prolonged freezing bath diminished his raging cockstand.

Thank you, Elderwood, Haig thought, watching Aislin try very hard to pretend not to stare at him. He drew out his frigid bath until he lost feeling in his toes, solely to enjoy her discomfort. She paced back and forth, delighting him with a 360-degree view of her body like a private fashion show. Her face was flushed—whether from embarrassment or desire, he couldn't tell, and didn't care. The rosy tint in her cheeks just added to her appeal. A hint of warmth in the ice queen. The smallest bit of innocence in the warrior savage. And damned if he'd ever seen a more arousing sight.

He flexed a little more than necessary for her benefit. Made sure to wash *everywhere.* Hygiene was important. And all the while, Miss Butter Won't Melt In My Mouth But I'll Suck Your Tongue Like A Lollipop couldn't seem to find anything else to occupy her. Every once in a while she caught herself staring and scowled at him as if it was his fault. Haig just grinned wider. Stepping out of the creek, he made a show of stretching and twisting before he sauntered past her with his flag still flying high despite all half-hearted efforts to make it subside. When he pulled his spare clothes out of his saddlebag, Aislin made a sound of annoyance, turned her back to kneel, and dug her hands into a patch of loose dirt.

A better man would have given the poor girl a reprieve. Happily, no one ever expected *good* from Haig. Still, he might have left her to whatever ritual she felt the need to perform, but curiosity got the better of him. He dragged on his hunting gear without bothering to dry off. Dark pants, black linen shirt, and soft leather boots were his standard for any mission, but their patchy dye was best suited for an environment like the Elderwood where it acted like camouflage. "Whatcha doin'?"

"My job."

Raising an eyebrow, he ambled closer. She held perfectly still in a most awkward position on all fours, her eyes closed and her expression pinched with concentration. "Are you communing with earthworms?"

"*Shh!*"

Unable to resist, he came closer and peered at her forearms. She looked like she'd planted herself, but he could almost detect a faint magical glow. Holding a hand over hers, he felt the slightest…disturbance, like warm rabbit fur brushing across his palm.

All at once, his mind did that astral daydream thing and…

He was lying on a bed of soft moss beneath billions of stars and two massive moons so bright it almost felt like day. Aislin straddled him, her body arched, her head thrown back as she bucked her hips, riding him hard and fast. She was shameless, and utterly lost in her own pleasure, one tattooed hand stroking between her legs, the other toying with her pierced nipple.

Haig's fingers itched to join in the play, but the wicked Huntress had trussed him up with leather straps, leaving him completely at her mercy. Breath left him in stunned wonder.

Aislin ground her hips down on him, bringing herself to orgasm, and he groaned, wanting desperately to have her closer, to feel her body quiver in his arms. Oh, but the sight of her pleasure… Hold fast, he told himself. It's only her first. They still had hours left for this game; he couldn't let it end too soon. Haig clutched his binds, strained against them until leather bit into his wrists, hoping the pain would keep his own climax at bay. Only her first…

Then she fell forward, catching herself against his chest and gave him a purely bedroom smile that made Haig want to put her on her back and pound into her until she melted completely. It was a sated smile, yet hungry at the same time. Like a cat who'd had a taste of fresh cream and wanted more. He bucked up, savoring her gasp, the way her eyelids lowered to half-mast. Aislin caught her lower lip between her teeth, slowly let it slide free, wet and reddened from the heat of her mouth. Like a man dying of thirst, he strained up to taste it for himself.

Aislin met him halfway, kissed him even as her hips rocked on him. Haig yanked hard on his binds. They wouldn't budge. He growled his frustration, nipped her tongue. "Release me," he demanded.

In response, she shifted up his cock until it slid almost completely free of her, then slowly took him all the way back in. Gods, this was torture!

Then she whispered against his lips, "I love the way you feel inside me…" And he shouted with the force of an orgasm he had no hope of holding back any longer.

Haig sucked in a harsh breath, his skin heating and prickling with awareness.

To his surprise, Aislin went rigid, as if she'd felt it, too. Suddenly, she shoved to her feet, pulling free of the ground so fast, dirt kicked up all over him. "Get some sleep," she ordered. "This won't be a short journey."

"And you know this because the earthworms told you?" Shit, he sounded like he really had just had a screaming orgasm instead of just dreaming one.

She ignored him.

Still mired in the aftereffects of his vision, Haig didn't have the stamina to push for more information. He laid out his pallet and made himself as comfortable as a man could be on the ground without shelter. At least the night was warm enough that they wouldn't need a fire and the sky was glittering with stars, not a raincloud in sight.

Aislin blew out the lanterns and settled in as far away from him as the clearing would allow. Haig let the silence stretch for a few more minutes before he said, "You're still thinking about that kiss, aren't you?" He was. Or he would have been if he didn't have that vision making reruns in his mind. *Down!*

"Yes, I often like to relive my past mistakes just as I'm ready to go to sleep."

"Lots of people do," he replied gravely. "But don't beat yourself up too hard. We make mistakes so we can learn from them. Now you know the next time I'm two minutes away from making you come harder than you've ever come in your life, the correct response is to take off your clothes, not throw me in the creek."

"You. Are. Insufferable!"

Haig grinned. Oh yeah, she wanted him. And not only in his dreams, either. He just had to make her see it. "It's not too late to change your mind." Having never been in a situation like this, Haig was unfamiliar with this aggravating ache in his balls, but for some odd reason, he almost enjoyed it, knowing Aislin had to be feeling it, too. He readjusted his crotch. Maybe not as acutely, but still.

As if to prove him right, Aislin turned over, then back again. She huffed, rustled her pallet, got up and dragged it over a few inches.

Five minutes later she was dragging it right back again.

Trying very hard not to laugh, Haig offered, "Would you like to pick up where we left off?"

"I would sooner eat a pine cone than let you touch me again!"

"Hey, lady, *you* straddled *me*, remember? And who said anything about touching you?"

He could practically hear her frown in the baffled silence that followed. "Are you messing with me again?"

Abandoning all pretense of sleep, Haig sat up and faced her. "I'll make you a deal. I bet I can get you to orgasm without ever laying a finger on you. No magic, no tricks." Aislin scoffed, but she didn't tell him to fuck off. He took that as the opening it obviously was. She was intrigued. "If I win, you'll thank me—" He ducked the rock she threw at his head with a fraction of an inch to spare. "Fine. If I win, you'll tell me what you were doing back there with the dirt earlier."

"You can't make a woman orgasm without physical contact. This is just another ruse. You think you'll get me to lose my head and—"

"Then bet me. Name your terms. If you don't think I can do it, then you have nothing to lose."

Silence. Then: "*When* you lose, you'll start taking this mission seriously."

This was in the bag. "You assume I don't?"

"You'll stop treating me as one of your sluts and start giving me the respect I deserve."

He groaned. "Since when are respect and sexual interest mutually exclusive?"

"Do you agree or not?"

Female logic just wasn't meant to be understood by men. "I agree," he begrudged.

"Then I guess we have a bet."

"I guess so."

"So… How do we…do this?"

He grinned, prowling over to her. "Just lie back and close your eyes, baby. I'll do the rest."

CHAPTER 4

Aislin eyed him warily as he came to her. He moved like a panther on the prowl, head canted low, shoulders working up and down, and he was completely silent in his advance.

Her heart pounded, her knees pressed together as Haig settled on his side so close to her she felt the heat of his skin and smelled the earthy scent of him. Moss and healthy male. Aislin squirmed an inch farther from him, lay flat on her back like a plank of wood.

"Relax," he said. "I won't touch you. Close your eyes."

After a moment, she did.

He was silent for so long, she thought he'd fallen asleep. She even began to relax a little, certain this little bet was the most ridiculous thing in the world. Of course he'd lose. This momentary embarrassment would be worth it to gain the respect she wanted. Better yet, she'd be able to hold his failure over his head forever after. Aislin liked that quite a bit.

Haig breathed out slowly against her temple. "I love women who dress in leather," he said. "It's earthy, and just a little naughty at the same time. It hugs you so well you might as well be naked, but hides all the sweetest parts of you and dares a man to touch." His voice rumbled low, almost like a comforting croon, but his words… "It's the laces," he confided at her ear. "Nothing sexier than tugging on the ends, pulling them loose one grommet at a time.

"I almost had you there before, too. If you hadn't stopped me, I would have taken my time with you. You don't unwrap a present that sweet in a hurry. You savor it, build the anticipation. Inch by square inch."

Just like before, Aislin was struck with that odd sense of familiarity. Less than a minute into his game, she felt as if they'd done this thousands of times before. Her body responded to the sound of his voice as if he'd trained it; her mind painted pictures from his words, her internal gaze following where he led. She pictured his fingers at the laces of her bodice, tugging them free; almost felt the night air on her overheated skin, his touch, his kiss. Haig hadn't laid a single finger on her, but Aislin's breath caught the same way it had when she'd been in his lap.

"I would peel the leather off your shoulders first, kiss the places where the seams dug into your skin just a little too hard. Then I'd pull it down lower to the peaks of your breasts. I'd keep you there a while. Your arms would be pinned to your sides so you couldn't stop me, and I'd feast on you as long as I liked. Your skin's so soft, Aislin, it tastes so sweet, I can't get enough."

Aislin licked her lips. They felt swollen, eager for his kisses.

"I'd kiss your chest, push your breasts up and lick the top swells, trail down into the valley between them. You'd try to reach for me, to make me go faster, but you couldn't. Your hands wouldn't go higher than my waist, so you'd clutch there, grinding down on me, and I'd let you. You'd be aching by then, but those pants of yours wouldn't allow enough freedom to find release. You'd need me for that."

Aislin's fingers curled into fists at her sides. She fought to keep her breathing even, to disguise the effect he was having on her, but he seemed to know anyway.

He leaned closer, his mouth almost to her temple and kept going, his voice lowered to a wicked whisper. "You'd buck up to free your breasts and demand I kiss them properly and oh, baby, how I would. I'd suck on your nipple until it was hard, then suck harder to drive you crazy. I'd use my teeth just enough to get a shiver out of you, maybe take a little nip. And I'd do the same to the other one, and you'd writhe in my arms so hard I'd have to pin you down to keep you still. I'd put my hands on your ass—gods, what a sweet ass you have. I'd knead and massage, all the while pressing you down on me, back and forth. Back…and forth."

Aislin disguised her shiver by turning on her side to face him. Eyes closed, she clutched at the pallet beneath her to keep from reaching for him. Already she was all but panting, moisture gathering between her legs. She tried to think of something else, but there was no escaping Haig's voice.

"It wouldn't be enough for you. You'd want me on top of you, inside you. You'd try to touch me, but by then I'd be a hair trigger, so I'd put you in the softest patch of grass, kiss down your stomach to your belly button, tease you until I had your pants undone. You'd be eager to get out of them, but leather is tricky. I probably wouldn't get them lower than your knees."

He shifted around, mouth skimming across her hair just barely. Aislin could have called him on it, but she made the mistake of opening her eyes. In the low light of the moon, she saw he was gripping his hard cock as if he couldn't help himself.

"I'd push them down just a little farther so I could get my hand between your legs. You'd be slick, dripping wet for me. I'd be aching to taste you, but not yet. I'd want to see you get wild first, hear you plead for me." His fist pumped up and down once, twice. Aislin couldn't look away, crossing her legs as she hunched in on herself. A small moan escaped her. *Look away!*

As if he sensed her staring and knew she wanted to balk, Haig murmured, "It's okay, Aislin, I want you to look." He shifted a little to allow the moonlight to better illuminate him, and he kept stroking. "Gods, just the thought of your wet pussy makes me so hard it hurts. I'd rub the sweet little nub of your clit, dip just the tip of my finger inside you. Then I'd push deeper and circle your clit with my thumb. I'd fuck you with just my fingers, slow and long at first, then hard and fast." He stroked himself faster and tension coiled low in Aislin's belly. She'd never seen anything as erotic as this. Her inner muscles tensed, clenching on emptiness. "You wouldn't be so quiet then. You'd beg me to fill you more, to give you all of this, and don't stop. Never stop. And I'd want to so badly…"

Aislin drew her knees up higher, panting, watching him stroke himself and imagining that cock pushing inside her, stretching and filling her. She ached for it. Her breasts felt fuller, trapped inside her bodice, and she wanted it off.

"But first I'd want to taste you. I'd put my mouth on you, suck your clit in time with my fingers. By then you'd be out of your head, clutching my hair and moaning my name and you'd have no idea how much that affected me." He groaned, arm muscles twitching as his stroking hand paused at the base. Breathing hard, he whispered, "I'd keep you on the edge for at least an hour." The stroking resumed and Aislin shuddered, riveted. She was so close, a single touch would set her off and, gods, it looked like he was, too. His voice got lower, rougher, his harsh breaths stirring the hair at her temple.

"You'd strain for it at first, try to force me to go faster, make you come." At the last word, his entire body twitched and Aislin tensed, quivering, riding the edge of orgasm. "But after a while, you'd be reduced to lying pliant in my arms, at my mercy, pleading for release. I'd know the moment you couldn't possibly take anymore, and then I'd *make* you take more, stroke you deeper, faster, suck you hard and long until your thighs clenched around me and you arched up off the ground…*and shattered.*"

He whispered the last right by her year, his mouth barely skimming the lobe and it was enough to push her over the edge. Aislin sucked in a breath, but couldn't bite back a moan as her body clenched in a sudden, powerful orgasm that pulled her knees up to her chest and made her shudder.

"Ah, gods, that's it." He grunted, wide shoulders twitching as he stroked himself to come in hard spurts on the ground next to her. She lay there dazed for a long time, her pleasure somehow heightened by the sight of his. The bet won, Haig leaned down and rested his forehead against her temple, as if he was too worn out to keep his head upright anymore. Still stroking himself slowly, he murmured, "And, baby, that's just what I can do with my mouth," and set her off all over again.

Haig felt no satisfaction over winning their little bet. He'd expected it, had been prepared to gloat over how easily he'd managed to wring not one but two orgasms from her, but instead all he felt was a dazed sort of wonder. He'd played this trick on other women in the past—it was a handy skill to have. But never before had he reacted to it the way he had with Aislin.

Every time her breath hitched, every time her hands clenched and her body swayed toward him, Haig had struggled to control the impulse to pull her into him and do all the things he'd said he would. Somehow, as hard as saying the words had made him come, as amazing as his vision had felt, he knew it wouldn't hold a candle to the act itself.

Deeply perturbed by the revelation of this inexplicable weakness, he stayed next to Aislin for a long time, savoring the sound of her breaths, before he finally made himself get up and return to his own pallet.

Aislin didn't say a word. He wanted her to, needed a caustic retort from her to get his head right again, but she stayed silent. After a while, she sighed and rolled over to face away from him, feigning sleep. Haig almost smiled. Let her pretend. No doubt she thought if she stalled long enough, he'd forget their bargain and let her keep her secrets. *No such luck, my sweet.* He'd get to the bottom of every single one of them before this assignment was through.

For now, he stayed silent, watching the moon's slow progress across the sky. It took a long time, but eventually his eyelids became heavy and sleep pulled him under.

In his dreams, Aislin bathed naked in the stream, water glistening on her skin, nipples beaded hard from the cold. She smiled coyly and crooked a beckoning finger for him to come to her. And like a besotted, teenage fool, he did.

CHAPTER 5

Something nudged against Haig's foot. He frowned at being disturbed from sleep but, unwilling to give in to the rude awakening, he didn't respond.

He was almost asleep again when he heard a soft whistle. Grumbling, he rolled over, determined to ignore the intrusion.

That's when his foot got kicked hard.

"Bloody fucking hell, woman, can you not see I'm sleeping?" Haig sat up, squinted against the sun's glare at the roundish shadow standing over him. "You don't look like my woman." He rubbed sleep from his eyes and took a better look. It definitely wasn't Aislin. As the shape of a rotund ruffian with a ridiculously bushy beard came into focus, he noticed other discrepancies, too. Beardie had four friends lounging around the glen, one of them pointing Aislin's crossbow at her where she sat against a tree. She didn't look happy about the situation. *That makes two of us.*

"So I ask m'self," Beardie wheezed, "wot's a pretty gel like that doin' wit the Wraith in my woods? An' then I sees is the bloody 'untress darkenin' my glen. Wit the bloody Wraith. None too friendly wit ye, in' she? But there ye both are. In my woods. Now why's tha' be, eh? You tell me tha'. Now."

Haig stared at him. It'd sounded like words, he was almost sure of it. But damned if he could make any sense of them.

"Wot're ye doin' in my *glen*!"

Haig snapped his fingers. "Glen! I understood glen."

Beardie pointed to his associate. "Shoot 'er in the leg."

"What?" Aislin snapped.

Haig shot forward, slammed into Beardie's gut and drove him to the ground. Before the rest of the ruffians had had a chance to register what happened, Haig drew one of Beardie's knives and shoved the blade against his neck. Or his beard where his neck should be.

Beardie wheezed a laugh, baring brown teeth covered with foul-smelling muck. "Five 'gainst two, mate. She'll be dead 'fore ye can spit."

"You think so? Look again." He allowed Beardie just enough breathing room to turn his head. As he'd known she would, Aislin had disarmed the man who'd taken her weapon and now had him beneath her boot with the crossbow pointed at another of their gang.

Beardie chuckled, but some of his confidence had waned. "Means noffin'. Me men are *profes'nals*."

Against all sense of self-preservation, Haig leaned into Beardie's putrid breath to whisper, "And I'm the fucking Wraith."

Beardie blanched. His chubby cheek twitched nervously, eyes darting as he comprehended his predicament. "Can't 'urt us in the glen," he argued desperately. "Is forbidden."

"Can't *spill blood* in the glen, true," Haig allowed. "But that still leaves an awful lot of ways I can inflict all kinds of pain on you and your men."

Beardie seemed to consider that. After a moment he scowled and ordered, "Stan' down."

The ruffians backed up a step.

"Ash, my love, what do you think?"

"I don't trust them," she said, having made no move to release her prey.

Haig studied Beardie's ugly mug, then shrugged. "I think they're okay." He pushed off and got up, waiting patiently as Beardie wobbled his way to his feet, as well.

With a curt nod that might have been thanks, the apparent gang leader pointed at the knife Haig had liberated from him. "Tha's mine, i' is."

Haig smiled. "That remains to be seen."

Beardie drew himself up and stuck his hands into his pockets. "Aye, well… Fine."

"Now," Haig said, "what say we all sit down and talk like civilized human beings, eh?"

Beardie nodded to his men, and all of them, with the exception of the one still under Aislin's heel, obediently sat in a circle on the ground. Beardie followed suit, which obligated Haig and Aislin to reciprocate. After a wordless battle of glares and head shakes, the two of them put their weapons aside and sat.

Haig spoke first. "Would you like to start by introducing yourselves?" He kept his gaze on Beardie.

"Me name's Troll," the gang leader answered.

Haig had to bite his tongue at that answer. "It's a pleasure to meet you, Troll." Nope. Couldn't let it lie. "Troll? Really? That's your name?"

"Aye," the man replied with an offended scowl. "What of it?"

Haig held his hands up in surrender. "All right, no need to get testy."

Troll's face turned ruddy, mouth twisting in distaste. "Wot're you doin' in me woods?"

"Passing through," Haig answered.

Troll snorted. "Aye, 'sright. The Wraith jus' passin' through the Elderwood. An' me mum's the queen, she is."

"What business is it of yours why we're here?" Aislin asked.

"I don' give a bloody frig why's you're 'ere 'untress," Troll spat back. "You're as much a woodsman as your blessed father, may the dirt be light on 'im. But you don't 'unt wit company. An' no one brings the Wraith 'long wot don' got reason to."

Aislin frowned. "What's this Wraith thing you keep talking about?"

Troll did a double take at her. "*Wot's this Wraith thing?*" He speared Haig with a sharp look, but spoke to the Huntress in suddenly guarded tones. "Mistress Aislin, you keep dangerous company. All the worse for not knowin' the viper you bed down wit." Then he narrowed his eyes at Haig. "You're the queen's dog, you are. 'ave been since the war."

Haig said nothing.

"Aye, that gel knows just where the secret folk lie 'idden, don' she? Got 'erself a 'untress to flush 'em out an' the blood Wraith 'isself to take 'em down. Tidy little arrangement, in' it?" He gave Aislin a taunting grin. "An' 'ow many foal will ye be trussin' up for the fairest of 'em all, eh?"

Aislin frowned at Haig.

"One target," he answered for them. "Hardly worth the mention. We'll be out of your hair before you know it and no one will miss us when we're gone."

Troll snorted and spat a wad of brownish gunk on the ground. Droplets of it stuck in his beard and Haig gagged. "Right wit that ye are." Troll's beady eyes gleamed suddenly and a crooked smile hooked his mouth. "I says one word to the wind, I do, an' your foal will skitter aways so far 'e'll never be caught 'gain. Wot will ye give me to 'old me peace?"

"I'll let you live," Haig replied.

Troll's smile fell away in a hurry. "Aye, well… Fine." He spat again. "Bloody rotten business wit the Wraith prowlin' in me bushes."

So wrong…

"One week," Troll offered magnanimously. "Won't say 's I saw noffin', 'less someone asks. But I won't lie, neither."

"Can I trust your men to hold to that?"

Troll looked over his men, got a nod from each. "Aye, you can, at that."

"Then it appears our business is concluded. Do we part as friends, Troll?"

The gang leader didn't miss the subtle threat in those words. His eyes widened as he climbed to his feet in a hurry, tumbling back down twice before he found his balance. "Friends, aye. All the 'wood's friend to the Wraith. Gods be wit ye both. Good day. Men! Onward! An' leave the 'orses alone, ye daft buggers! Friends don' steal from the 'untress an' 'er companion! Where's your manners? *Git!*"

Aislin watched the comedy of criminals depart, thoroughly confused by what had just taken place. Never before had she been accosted in the Elderwood like this. On the rare occasion when she did come across people, they always deferred to her with the respect they showed to one of their own.

And Haig! What in the world was a Wraith, and why would a band of thieves be so terrified of him? Just what exactly had he done to earn his name during the war? Aislin wasn't a fool; she'd known this mission wouldn't be a diplomatic envoy, but now she had to wonder what Snow White was up to, sending her into the Elderwood with what seemed to be her best assassin. Who could be important enough—dangerous enough—to warrant this kind of effort?

When Troll and his band were gone, Haig got up, dusted himself off, and set about rolling up his pallet as if nothing was wrong. Aislin followed suit, but questions nagged at her. She didn't like secrets, especially when everyone except her already seemed to know them. Their camp broken up, they refilled their water bottles in the creek. Aislin tried to read Haig's expression, but he acted as if the last half hour hadn't happened at all.

"I assume you have a direction for us to head in," he said.

Aislin nodded. "Northeast. We have at least a two days' ride before I can narrow it down more."

"Then let's go."

He rummaged in his saddlebag and extracted two chunks of dried meat and some wafers to share between them for a breakfast meal, but they didn't linger in the glen to eat it. Aislin contented herself to eat in silence for a while, but once she was finished, her curiosity got the better of her. She turned to Haig, a slew of questions on the tip of her tongue.

"Ah-ah," he said before she'd said a word. "We had a bet. And as I recall, it was for your secrets, Huntress, not mine." He crooked his finger in a come-hither gesture for her to start talking.

Aislin turned away so he wouldn't see her flush. "The bet wasn't fair," she muttered.

"Would you like to try again? Double or nothing?"

"No!"

Haig chuckled. "You don't know what you're missing."

That had become painfully clear to her last night. She'd underesti-mated him and it had cost her dearly. To her shame, it hadn't ended when Haig had returned to his own pallet. What he'd said to her had plagued her all night long. She'd slept fitfully, her dreams filled with lurid images and tactile sensations making her most sensitive parts throb with acute awareness that the source of her frustration and the key to its relief lay a few scant feet away. Aislin hated how at ease he seemed when she could barely meet his gaze for more than a second.

"I have all day, you know." How could he look so…*happy*?

"I…" Gods, this was hard. Before his death, her father had been adamant that no one ever find out about her Gift. With Queen Zora-na actively seeking out anyone with even a smidgen of controllable raw magic, the danger had been too great. Had she ever learned what Aislin could do, the evil queen wouldn't have hesitated to take ad-vantage.

Isn't that what Snow White is doing now? an insidious voice of doubt whispered in her mind.

No, she couldn't believe that. In the year since Snow had taken the throne, she'd been nothing but just and fair to all of her subjects. She'd even been lenient to Zorana's old supporters, when any other regent would have had the lot of them executed at once. At her core, Snow White was honorable and kind. Aislin had to believe that, otherwise she'd never be able to live with herself for taking this assignment.

As if he could hear her thoughts, Haig leaned sideways in his sad-dle and reached over to touch her hand. "It's all right. The war is over, you're safe now."

Looking into his eyes, some of her apprehension eased. Despite knowing better, Aislin felt safe with Haig. That should have put her on guard right then and there, shut her up and slammed the door on the topic. Instead, Aislin found herself confiding in him. "It's how I track: I sense energy and intent. Doesn't matter who or what the target is, as long as someone wants it found, the intent alone creates a direct trail. It's like an invisible map in the earth's ley lines, and I can read it."

Haig whistled. "No wonder you didn't want to tell me. If I could do that…"

"What *can* you do? There has to be something besides… I mean, the queen picked you for a reason—"

"Have you ever heard the expression 'Don't ask questions you don't want answered'?"

"If I didn't want answers, I wouldn't ask."

Haig grinned. "Fair enough."

When he didn't say anything more, she raised an eyebrow. "Well?"

"All in good time, sweetest. All in good time."

And for the next three hours, he didn't say another word.

CHAPTER 6

An unexpected storm forced them to seek shelter shortly after midday. Between one hour and the next, the sky had turned dark and opened up in a massive downpour. They were both soaked through by the time they managed to pitch a small shelter and with nothing dry to burn for a fire, it promised to be a miserable few hours until the storm subsided.

"Trust you to take advantage of the situation," Aislin groused when Haig brushed shoulders with her.

He barked a laugh, shivering with cold. "I can say with ninety percent certainty that this is one situation where sex is the very last thing on my mind."

"But you're still thinking about it, right?" Her teeth chattered.

Still grinning, Haig bumped his shoulder against hers. "You're beginning to understand me." He shuddered, rubbing his arms vigorously. "But you know, it's probably best if we get naked."

Aislin peeked out at the sky. "It's just a brief squall. It'll pass in a minute."

As if to mock her, lightning split the sky and a volley of hail the size of pheasant eggs bounced off the forest floor.

"Suit yourself," he said and put a few inches between them to shrug out of his shirt. He wrung out as much moisture as he could, then set it on a rock to dry while he struggled with his boots and pants. Aislin had seen him naked the night before, but somehow this was different. He wasn't preening, or drawing anything out to prolong her embarrassment. He was adroit and efficient, every movement rife with purpose that had nothing to do with seduction, but somehow all she could think about was putting her hands on him.

Haig was beyond handsome. His face had the classical symmetry of high art angel statuary, but his body was all earthy warmth. He had muscles hewn by hard work, not hours spent lifting weights. His skin was tan, lightly dusted with golden hair, his hands were callused, and his back was scarred. He could be graceful in a predatory way when necessary, but in unguarded moments he was more playful, almost clumsy, and utterly artless.

Aislin understood the appeal now, and wasn't surprised at all that so many women fell under his spell so eagerly. A vain man would set himself apart, stand back and bask in admiration. Haig was the opposite. He wanted to get as close as possible, and that was precisely what drew her. He was like a great big cat brushing around her, demanding to be petted and not particularly choosy about the method, as long as contact was involved.

"You're right." The words came out of her mouth before she could stop them, earning her a questioning look. "I think I am beginning to understand." And she doubted he'd like the conclusions she'd drawn.

"Does that mean you're getting naked, too?"

Aislin rolled her eyes. "You know I have to." Keeping her wet clothes on was the surest way to freeze to death. She tugged on the laces of her bodice, but to her dismay, they stuck, and her fingers were already numb, rendering them useless.

"Here, let me." Haig pinched one end between thumb and forefinger and yanked hard enough to loosen the knot. With quick movements, he pulled the length of lacing from the loops and set it aside. Aislin let him draw the garment from her completely, then raised her arms when he reached for the hem of her chemise. "Silk. I approve."

She didn't comment. Cotton was too thick to wear under leather for any length of time and wool was much too scratchy. Silk was the only fabric soft enough to protect her skin from chafing yet still thin enough to be unobtrusive. She winced a little when he pulled it off over her head and wadded it up in his fist to wring out.

Next came her pants. Soaked through, they were almost impossible to get off, but somehow they managed. When she was naked, Haig took her hands between his and chafed them, blowing on her fingertips for warmth. "How are your feet?"

"F-fine."

"Come here." He stretched out at the outer edge of their shelter and pulled her down to lie between him and the moss-covered back wall. They stuck together from chest to knee, shivering in the cold. "The leathers will take forever to dry," Haig said, rubbing her back. "Did you pack anything else?"

Aislin couldn't remember. She always had a change of clothes in her saddlebag but she never had reason to use them. At the moment she had a hard time recalling what exactly those clothes were. "Dunno," she said.

"'S all right. I don't mind you riding naked."

Aislin giggled, which set off a hard bout of shivers.

Haig moved in tighter so she was snugly sandwiched between him and the moss. It took a while, but eventually their shared body heat stopped the worst of her shivers and she regained feeling in her fingers and toes. "We should switch," she offered. Haig's back was to the storm; he was taking the worst of the cold.

He scowled. "I finally got you naked in my arms and you want me to move? Forget it."

"What do you mean, *finally*? You just met me yesterday!" And he'd already managed to get under her skin.

"Exactly my point. Usually by this time I've spent thirty hours like this and I'm putting my clothes back *on*."

"Thirty hours? As in three zero?" He had to be kidding.

Haig grinned. "Got you curious, don't I?"

"About thirty hours of sex? No, thanks. Not into that kind of pain."

His hand caressed a leisurely trail from her hip, up her spine to her nape and down to her hip again. "You just haven't met the right lover for it. You wouldn't feel a single ounce of pain with me. You might be sore as hell after, but I'd be, too. And that's not pain in the strictest sense."

"Splitting hairs now?"

"Toeing a fine line." And he followed the words with action, tickling her foot with his toe. "Besides. I'd be more than worth it."

She sighed. "If I wasn't so comfortable, I'd push you out into the storm."

He flashed her a boyish grin. "I'd just take you out with me."

There was laughter in Aislin's eyes, a genuine warmth he hadn't seen before, and with his hand on the swell of her ass, Haig hesitated, conscious of a fragile truce that had taken hold between them. He almost held his breath, waiting for her to end the moment with one of her verbal barbs, but she stayed silent.

Aislin lay in his arms with nothing but a structure of twigs and moss to keep the sky from falling down on them, and he'd never seen her more at ease. This was her element; she was wholly at home in nature, and the walls she'd built up in the city were finally starting to come down. Something told Haig he might never get her like this again once the mission was done and they returned to Kesteran. What a shame…

And all the more reason not to waste a single moment.

He traced her brow with a gentle fingertip. Her lashes fluttered like butterfly wings against his skin, and Haig felt something frighteningly akin to awe. Leaning in to claim a kiss, he stopped with his lips a hair's breadth from hers. *Wait… Wait…* He almost smiled when Aislin closed the distance and sealed their lips. The Huntress needed to hunt. And Haig was more than willing to let himself be chased.

He let her lead, accepted her kiss without giving much in return. As she grew bolder, more frustrated with his lack of response, Aislin pressed closer to him, threw a leg over his hip, strained back to drag more of his weight over her. For every mile she wanted, Haig gave an inch. He leaned over her just enough to keep her off balance, resisting the urge to put her on her back and cover her completely. He licked into her mouth with teasing swipes of his tongue, staying aloof even when she sucked on it to draw him deeper. His hands remained motionless at her back, even though it caused him physical pain not to palm her curves, delve between her legs to find out if she was as wet as he imagined.

His hips curled forward, but he stilled them, waiting for her to come to him. She didn't disappoint, rocking against him, aligning with him so well his dick rode the valley between the lips of her sex. Haig's breath caught to feel her hot and soaking wet against him—and that was before she reached down to claw his ass.

Aislin moaned, a sound of frustration rather than pleasure. The friction between them wasn't nearly enough to satisfy her—Haig made sure of that. No quickies for either of them this time, he wanted this to last. He needed Aislin to need him, not just want him, and he needed her to be the one to make the first move. Anything less than that and she'd blame him for the whole encounter and dismiss it, along with him.

Her hand slid up his back, fingers tangling in his hair. Then she curled them and gave a yank to pull him away. "Are you done playing your games yet?"

Haig gave her his most innocent look. "Who, me? I'm just lying here." To prove his point, he stretched out on his back and put his hands under his head. "In fact, I'm tired. I think I should catch a few winks before we head out again."

His mouth quirked when he closed his eyes, shutting out the bafflement on her face. *Take the bait, sweetheart. You know you want to.*

She made him wait a long time, no doubt inwardly debating strategy. He never heard her move, but he sensed her. His skin prickled with goose bumps when she moved closer. She was heat and energy hovering over him two seconds before her hands touched the ground by his ears and she leaned over low enough for her breasts to rub against him. Haig bit back a groan, dug his heels into the dirt. The teasing witch nipped his lower lip, then trailed kisses across his jaw and neck, but kept her hips to herself.

She nuzzled against his chest, licked his nipple, grazed her teeth across it, and Haig's eyes almost rolled back in his head. He breathed in deep and slow, as if that would prevent her from hearing the rapid thump of his heart. From the way he felt her smile against his sternum, she knew exactly what she was doing to him and she liked it.

Haig endured the sensual torture with stubborn stoicism. He fisted his hands and refused to touch her when she brushed her knuckles down his side, across his abdomen and down his inner thigh. He didn't react when she clamped her thighs around his hips—her core still hovering just out of reach, damn her! And no matter how much his mouth watered for them, he didn't kiss the swells of her breasts when she cruelly smothered his face between. "Enjoying yourself, are you?" he asked.

Aislin hummed, her hips coming down briefly on his stomach, and he mindlessly thrust up before he could stop himself. "Aren't you?" she returned, curling her spine so her pussy rubbed back and forth against him. Several inches off the damned mark. This was torture.

"Immensely," he grated.

Aislin raised up, and all he could feel was the taunting nearness of her body and one hand caressing his cheek. "Poor Haig," she whispered at his ear, her hand trailing down his chest to his stomach, then lower, across his loins. Close enough to torment, but far enough to avoid even an accidental graze against his rock-hard dick. "If you wanted to win, you shouldn't have tipped your hand."

Haig's eyes snapped open to find her already retreating to her place next to him. He followed instantly, insinuating himself between her thighs before she had a chance to deny him. And as he stared down at her expression of pure triumph, Haig came to the unsettling discovery that this might be one game he wouldn't win.

And the worst part was: he didn't want to.

"You really shouldn't pull the tiger's tail, sweetheart."

She raised an eyebrow. "Is that so? What will he do? Bite me?"

Sounded like a good idea to him! Haig brought his face to her shoulder and sank his teeth into the muscle where it met her neck. She yipped in surprise, arching her hips up for him and this time he took the invitation. Eagerly. Propped on one elbow, he gripped her hip with his free hand to keep her still and buried himself inside her with one, long thrust.

His entire body went taut, and his jaw slackened. He didn't dare breathe too deeply for fear of going off before they'd even gotten started. Her body clamped down on him, soft heat pulling him deeper, and for a moment, the legendary seducer couldn't think. All of his bed tricks, all of his expertise, all of the suave witticisms he usually shuffled like a pack of cards, were gone.

Aislin hooked a leg over his hips, put her arms around him, digging her nails into his shoulders. She arched her back, pressing her breasts against him, and Haig lost his ever-loving mind.

Aislin felt Haig's groan reverberate through his chest. *Now you've done it.* She'd jumped in with both feet, and there was no going back.

And the worst part was: she didn't want to.

Haig pulled out slowly, then thrust back hard and fast, making her whole body jerk. Seated as deep inside her as he could get, he circled his hips a few times, stimulating her clit before he pulled back again and repeated the cycle. The rhythm he set was a teasing, maddeningly slow build. Each time he drove forward, Aislin gasped, thrilling at the way he filled her, the way his fingers dug into the soft flesh of her hip hard enough to ache and then released almost immediately. When he circled, her body hummed, quivering with anticipation. And each time he slowly pulled back, it drew her away from the edge just enough to hold off her orgasm without cooling her pleasure at all.

Aislin hovered in torturous limbo, pinned by his weight so she couldn't do anything to make him go faster. Breathing hard, she arched restlessly, raked her nails over his shoulders and back, even clawed his ass. She managed to elicit another of those panty-wetting groans, but the stubborn ox didn't alter his rhythm at all.

Growling in frustration, she nipped his shoulder. Haig sucked in a harsh breath, pulled back to see her face, his eyes staring expectantly into hers. He was waiting for something. But what?

Another deep thrust, harder, and Aislin's head fell back against the soft moss, her mouth going slack. She felt Haig's mouth on the underside of her chin, his tongue trailing down her throat to linger at her pulse. Hot breath seared her as he whispered something against her skin, too low for her to hear, and then he thrust again, making her gasp. A wanton moan threatened to make its way past her throat, but she bit it back.

Gods, this was too much. The pleasure was dizzying. She couldn't feel the ground beneath her anymore; the cold meant nothing on her overheated skin. There was only Haig, the drive of his hips, the thundering of his heart, the hard puffs of his breath against her. He switched arms, altering his angle and freeing the other hand to roam over her body.

By then, Aislin's skin was so sensitive, his touch raised goose flesh wherever it went. Another thrust and Aislin couldn't prevent a little squeak. It brought his head up, his blue gaze burning into hers. He traced the underside of her breast, then palmed the weight, his thumb rubbing back and forth over her nipple in time with his hips.

"Haig," she gasped out when he pinched her nipple and gave a light tug. Pleasure shot like lightning across nerve endings down to her pussy, enough to make her clench reflexively around him, but still not a true climax.

"*Yes.*" He did it again, and she went limp in his arms, legs falling open in heedless invitation.

"Oh gods, yes…" The breathless words rushing out of her seemed to make him mad. He drove into her harder, faster. No more teasing, no more drawn-out pauses, Haig fucked her exactly as she needed. "Yesyesyesyes*yes! Haig!*"

He sealed his mouth over hers to smother her shout as the most exquisite pleasure shivered up her spine. Her body clenched hard, legs locked around him to keep him with her, and she was only dimly aware that he held himself deep inside her, doing that circling thing against her clit that kept the pleasure waves rocking through her entire body. She wasn't quite finished coming when he started to move again and the slow back-and-forth friction sent pleasant zings through her to ease her down from the clouds—but not all the way.

Within moments he had her on that brink once more, building her up with languorous strokes and pulling back. She frowned at him. "Haig?"

Staring at her, his only response was, "Again." He hiked her hip up higher, altered his angle a fraction of an inch, but that small change had him thrusting against the most heavenly spot ever bestowed upon a woman. Aislin moaned loudly, which seemed to inflame him even more. He pushed a little harder, a little faster, wrenching mindless cries from her until she once again screamed his name as she shattered into a million pieces.

"Again," he whispered against her throat, reaching down to rub her clit as he continued fucking her in a relentless drive that sent Aislin out of her head. She clung on to him for her sanity as a mad litany of words spilled from her mouth, words she never would have said under normal circumstances. She begged him, she pleaded, she threatened, and then she prayed. Not to the gods, but to Haig. He tasted each word with his mouth against her throat as he continued to move inside her, over her, wringing more and more pleasure from her, and each time only allowed her to come down for a second before demanding, "Again." Again, again, and again, until she lost all track of time; didn't know whether the flashes of light floating in her vision were fireflies or the result of an orgasmic break with reality. And she didn't care.

It went on for so long, Aislin forgot where she was. She couldn't move, the world was spinning and Haig was the only thing holding her together. Her voice had gone hoarse long ago, reduced to squeaks and moans but, as exhausted as she was, her body, now so attuned to Haig's expert handling, continued to writhe in helpless response, each climax bleeding into the next until all she knew was pleasure.

When she finally managed to focus on his face, he looked almost feverish, his eyes gleaming in triumph as he smiled and said, "Again…"

CHAPTER 7

Haig woke up to the sound of bird songs. He stretched before he opened his eyes, and groaned, aching all over. Only then did he register the chilled numbness in his fingers and toes and the soft, warm weight draped across his sternum. His eyes snapped open in an instant to look down at the woman sleeping soundly next to him.

It hadn't been a dream. Huh…

Aislin's face looked completely innocent in repose, her cheeks still flushed, her lips parted and a little dry. Poor darling. Haig had been relentless with her, determined to sear the day into her memory for all time. For some perverse reason, even knowing he'd likely never see her again once they parted ways, Haig had wanted that little part of her. He'd wanted a place in her memories, to be the reason she blushed and smiled when thinking back on her youth decades from now. It was stupid, but he couldn't have stopped himself if he'd tried. Which he rarely did, anyway.

Taking advantage of the peaceful moment, Haig studied her at his leisure. Her black hair was still in its braids, but deliciously mussed. She slept plastered to his side, but not clinging over him, as if even in sleep she held herself back. Her caramel skin gleamed with warmth in the early morning sun, inviting a man to touch and taste. She fit him almost too well, her curves molding to him like a puzzle piece.

"Beautiful," he whispered. Scooting down, he gently nudged her to lie on her back. She didn't wake, which meant he could play a little. *Excellent.* Licking his lips, Haig debated where to begin.

He brushed the backs of his fingers across her silky skin, loving the way she sighed in response. Her breasts were just the right size to overflow his hands bountifully without being obnoxious, and her nipples, a few shades darker than her skin were so damned responsive, he only had to circle them at a distance and they puckered eagerly, making his mouth water.

Never one to bother denying himself, Haig leaned down and took one into his mouth, sucking gently.

Aislin's breath came faster. He looked up to see if she was awake, but her eyes were still closed. He smiled. *Fair enough, I can try harder.* Moving over to the other breast, he lavished the same attention on it, delighted when her stomach muscles twitched a little beneath his hand when he used his teeth.

Still not waking up.

Was she playing with him?

Haig shrugged prosaically and kept going, pushing her breasts together and burying his face between them. He got a small moan in response, a subtle shift of her hips against him. Even in sleep, her body responded to him with an eagerness that made Haig feel like he'd been gifted with the greatest treasure on earth.

He knew she'd be too sore for another sexathon, but there were other things he could do—things he *should* do. It never hurt to be considerate of one's partner. He trailed kisses down her belly to the thatch of dark curls at the apex of her sex. He kissed the creases where her thighs met her torso as he gently spread her legs and settled between them.

"Haig?" she murmured. Definitely waking up now. The sound of her voice, still hoarse from screaming his name over and over last night made him go instantly hard. A man could get used to such a voice. He didn't check, but knew she was looking at him, half awake and likely confused. Understandable, given everything he'd put her through. Haig grinned and delved in for his morning feast.

Aislin gasped at the feel of his mouth against her. She moaned, her voice reedy, her body sore all over, and in one place especially. Her hands went to his head to push him away, but then he did something with his tongue that made her clutch him closer instead. He took full advantage, spreading her wide for his plundering mouth. He licked over her, into her, sucked her clit into his mouth, even nipped.

"Haig… oh gods…" She curled her hips up to him, legs opening and closing around his head. "Haig, please, I can't…"

"Easy," he said against her. "Don't strain for it. Let me give you what you need. That's it… that's it." Every touch, every kiss felt like praise. He was gentle, soothing her aching flesh with languorous laps, and when she climaxed, he pressed his tongue flat against her clit and licked her farther into ecstasy.

Afterward, he crawled back up over her body, kissing across her skin. When he reached her lips, she tasted herself on his tongue. "Good morning," he said, staring into her eyes. "How do you feel?"

"Hungry," she replied rolling them over until she was straddling him. Reversing the path he'd taken up her torso, she kissed her way down his, licking into the lines of his abs. His cock twitched against his abdomen and she couldn't wait to have a taste. Glancing up at Haig to gauge his reaction, she got a raised eyebrow in answer.

Aislin smiled. She made herself comfortable between his legs and took him in hand. He gasped. When she licked him from base to tip, he groaned, let his head fall back, but in the next instant he'd propped himself up to watch. For some reason, that made it even more delicious. She fisted her hand on him, pumped it up, drawing his foreskin over the head, then took just the tip into her mouth and sucked.

Haig cursed, bucked his hips up. She stayed him, kept sucking as she released his sheath to retreat and followed it down with her lips, taking him in as deep as she could. She savored the taste of him, pumping her hand over him as she lavished the head with wet, sucking tongue kisses that elicited a chorus of groans from him.

His hands cupped her face, clutched her braids and then let go, as

if he didn't trust himself that far. "Gods, Aislin… that's it. *Aahh, yes!*"
His pleasure made her want to give him more. She sucked harder,
pumped faster, delighting in the way his demands trailed off into
wordless grunts. Hefting his sac in her hand, she took him in deep,
then pulled back, hollowing her cheeks until he popped out of her
mouth with a loud smack. She took him right back in again, just as
deep, then let him slide free. On the third time, he sucked in a hard
breath. "So close…so…*gods yes!* About to…*come!*"

Aislin pumped her hand, sucked him hard, and swallowed him
down eagerly, until he reached down and pulled her up to crush her
in his arms. He kissed her in a deep, almost desperate assault on her
mouth, his hands shaking as they rubbed circles across her back.

For a long time, they just lay together, catching their breath and lis-
tening to the forest around them. Aislin had never felt so comfortable
in her entire life. But eventually, her body cooled, her mind regained
its power of higher thought, and she realized what she'd done.

She tensed, mortified, clueless about what to do next.

"Stop," Haig said.

"What?"

"You're overthinking it. Just relax for a while, enjoy the moment.
That's all it is."

For him, maybe. One conquest among many. Just another day in
the life of the whore. But Aislin was excruciatingly aware that she'd
just spent a night of insanely amazing sex with a man she'd met only
two days ago. A man she'd known would use her and discard her if
she let him, and she'd not only let him, she'd… Gods, she'd *pursued
him!* Aislin didn't remember much of the details of last night aside
from an endless series of toe-curling orgasms, but she did remember
him coming inside her. Twice.

Call her crazy, but Haig didn't seem like the type who'd stick
around to play daddy. And that wasn't even taking into consideration
any number of diseases he might be carrying from any number of
sexual partners.

He sighed. "You're still doing it."

Aislin pushed away and sat up, wincing at her aches and pains. She
needed a hot bath. What was she thinking? She needed a soul-deep

magical scrub to remove any and all evidence of Haig from her system. *Gods, what have I done?* She shoved to her feet, almost hitting her head on the roof of their shelter. "This never happened."

Haig snorted. "Like hell, it didn't."

"And it'll never happen again."

"We'll see," he returned after a contemplative pause. No anger, just a small smile and a calculating look. Probably already thinking about how to get her on her back again. She turned away, unable to stand the sight of him. Her face felt on fire, her hands were shaking; she wanted to be far, far away from here. The longer she stayed, the harder her teeth clenched and her throat caught with desperate tears.

She would *not* embarrass herself by crying in front of him like some damned virgin. No way would she give him the satisfaction of seeing how low he'd made her sink.

Because for just a moment there, she'd been almost… grateful.

Where were the horses? She whistled for Emer and went back to make a quick grab for her clothes, ducking away from Haig when he reached for her. Her leathers were still too wet to wear, but she pulled her chemise on to cover herself at least down to her hips. The thin armor was wholly insufficient against Haig's searing gaze. Just that look made her nipples bead against the silk. She gave him her back and he groaned, sending hot shivers up her spine. "We're not done discussing this," he said and she almost heard a frown in his voice.

Aislin ignored him and whistled again, gratified to hear pounding hoofbeats approach at a rapid clip a moment later.

Behind her, a rustle of movement told her Haig was getting up. "We still have a mission to complete. You can't just shut me out and pretend I don't exist."

Oh yes, she could. "I'm going to wash and dress. Start a fire if you can, we'll need a big breakfast before we set out." She didn't intend to stop again until they reached some kind of civilization. Obviously, being secluded with Haig like this was too dangerous.

"Aislin."

She swung into Emer's saddle to get away from him. "I'll be back soon." Bowing low over the mare's neck, Aislin kneed her into a gallop away from Haig. She didn't look back.

CHAPTER 8

Haig dressed himself, then dismantled the shelter and hunted down a handful of twigs dry enough to catch fire. He stoked it into a steady blaze, then busied himself preparing a quick, hearty meal of dried meats and cheeses, and a small pot of the strongest coffee he'd ever brewed, performing every single task with the mindless efficiency of muscle memory.

His mind, and every sense, physical or otherwise, was focused on just one thing: Aislin. He twitched at every rustle of sound, craning his neck to see if she was coming back. Each time the birds grew quiet overhead, he strained his ears for the sound of her approach.

He was tired, sore, and cranky as hell at the offhanded way she'd dismissed him, as if what they'd done together hadn't made one bit of difference at all. He'd never had a woman react to his lovemaking that way. It was pissing him off.

Haig scalded his mouth with a gulp of coffee, but savored the high-alert jitters of caffeine racing through his veins. He'd drained half the pot before recalling that he should probably save some for Aislin. Then he shrugged and drained the rest, wolfing down his portion of breakfast in a few bites.

But when his meal was done, a second pot of coffee brewed, and she still hadn't returned, Haig started to get worried. Tossing a few more twigs on the fire, he got up to pace, straining his eyes to see farther into the forest where she'd disappeared. She wouldn't have left him behind. No matter what was going through her mind, Aislin was still the Huntress commissioned by the queen to track down Haig's prey. She was just honorable enough to want to see it done, regardless of how much she didn't want to.

Yes, sooner or later, she'd come back.

And when she did, she'd get an earful from Haig about the stupidity of going off naked, barefoot, and alone through the gods-damned Elderwood!

Hoofbeats.

Haig took three steps in their direction before he stubbornly stopped himself. And then he saw her and swayed on his feet, almost tripping back onto the fire.

Aislin was draped in a simple, green dress with bell sleeves. The neckline was trimmed in brown leather, with laces crisscrossing down between her breasts. She'd left them loose, showing off an enticing shadow of cleavage. Her hair was loose, too. The thick, puffy waves flared out around her face like a lion's mane, tendrils curling around her chin and shoulders almost down to her waist. She walked with a delicate sway, toes first, her cheeks flushed angrily and her lips red and swollen from the night before.

And Haig couldn't remember what he'd been about to say.

She was walking Emer, some kind of weight draped over the saddle in her stead. She didn't say a word when she reached their camp, only spared him a quick glance, then turned to drag the sack from the saddle.

The back of her dress was crisscrossed with more lacing to make the cotton cling to her form. Any other woman would hold herself differently in a dress like that—they always did. Something about a lady's garments made women even more feminine, more graceful and fluid in movement. Not so with Aislin. She rolled up her sleeves, yanked her skirt out of the way, and crouched down in front of the sack, pulling out a large trout, four smaller river fish, and a knife.

He took the knife from her immediately. "Let me do that," he said.

"You don't want to ruin your pretty dress."

She handed it over without argument and whirled away to take a seat by the fire.

"There's fresh coffee in the pot, and the plate is yours. I already finished mine."

Aislin poured herself a cup and dug into her meal without a word. She ate quickly, polishing off the entire plate in a matter of minutes. Without a single word. She didn't even glance in his general direction. Not even when he started gutting the fish. He'd think she'd want to make sure Haig didn't ruin her catch.

Grinding his teeth, he quickly processed all five fish and stuck them onto sticks to bake over the fire. "How long do you intend to ignore me?" he asked, doing his damnedest not to sound bitter.

Aislin didn't say a word. She went out of her way to avoid his gaze, and in the process spotted her boots nearby. They should be almost wearable by now. His hadn't taken long to dry at all, but hers came up to her knee. Sexy as hell, but a pain in the ass when soaked through. Aislin retrieved them and pulled her skirt up over her knees to put them on. He'd had those legs wrapped around him all night long—he still felt where her heel had dug into his lower back. Where had that Aislin gone?

This version wasn't even the ice queen from before. She was just… ice. Stone-cold silence. And she managed to keep it up the whole time the fish cooked, and all through Haig's cutting them up into meal-sized pieces to take with them, and while they waited for the meat to cool, and longer still while they doused the fire, broke up camp, and mounted their horses.

"Where to?" he asked, certain that she'd at least answer work-related questions.

She didn't. Nudging Emer into a quick clip, she forced him to follow and trust that she was leading them true.

Haig sighed. It was going to be a very, very long trip.

Haig fell mercifully silent when they left camp. He didn't chatter, didn't press her, just kept pace with her, staring at her every few minutes. Aislin did her best to ignore him. While she'd bathed and fished, she'd made peace with her actions of last night. She'd told herself that Haig was a master seducer, and she'd resisted him as long as any other woman could have.

Yes, her weakness appalled her, but she couldn't bring herself to regret the night completely. She had enjoyed their time together—it'd be a lie and a disservice to them both to say otherwise. But Aislin also knew she couldn't risk falling into his seductive trap again. She wasn't like Haig; she couldn't keep her heart separate from her body. Sex meant something to her and since it obviously didn't to him, the only way this could end between them was in heartbreak—hers.

Haig was too strong a lure to risk eyeing, even at a distance. He just had to look at her, quirk his mouth in that little half-smile he had, and Aislin wanted to kiss him senseless. His voice shivered through her, reminding her of the things he'd whispered in her ear that first night. His touch rekindled the fire he'd started yesterday—it had never banked completely. Aislin walked the edge of a razor blade, acutely aware of every flick of his wrist on Romper's reins, every deep intake of breath as he savored the scent of rain and earth. She felt his gaze on her constantly and knew that the moment he crooked his finger for her, or even opened his arms in invitation, she'd dive into them without hesitation.

And she'd regret it for the rest of her life. A man like Haig wasn't built to be a footnote. He was an era, an epoch that would change her for all time. If Aislin let him in, he'd mold her soul to match him, and if he left her after that, she'd never be able to find her footing again.

So when he rode up beside her, when he nudged Romper so close their legs almost touched, Aislin kicked Emer into a gallop and left him to follow again. It was the only way she could keep breathing.

They rode for hours without saying a word. Haig shifted in his saddle, obviously eager to stop for a spell, rest up before they moved on, but Aislin ignored his discomfort and her own. They were only a few miles away from the village of Acorn and she desperately needed to get there. With other people around, other women to keep Haig busy, she might be able to relax long enough to track their next leg of the journey. No matter how unsettled Haig made her feel, they still had a mission to complete.

Finally, the forest gave way to a small wheat field. On the other side of it, the cottages of Acorn huddled together like frightened children along a single street lit with torches, and each window flickered with candlelight. Aislin didn't stop until they'd reached the inn. It didn't even have a name, being the only one around for miles, but they had a sturdy stable and comfortable beds. Not to mention, they could trade a couple of trout for rooms and a meal. The innkeeper was a stout, old man who made an excellent venison stew, and Aislin was starving for proper, hot food.

Aislin left Haig to take care of the horses while she went to make arrangements with the innkeeper. The main room was half-filled with travelers, locals, and a number of scantily clad wenches. No doubt as soon as they saw Haig, they'd take him off her hands. She was counting on it, eager for a few hours of peace and quiet. The thought of the gaudy women with their breasts almost hanging out putting their hands all over him didn't bother her at all. Good riddance.

The innkeeper was only too happy to accommodate them. "I've got one room free," he was saying as Haig made his entrance.

"That'll suffice," Haig replied, staring at Aislin until her cheeks felt burning hot. He didn't glance at the wenches behind him a single time, or even look at the innkeeper as he produced a gold coin for him from his pocket.

"At your service, sir," the innkeeper said with a pleased smile—and no wonder; Haig had just tipped him four times the cost of their room! "Will you be wishing for a repast? A bath?"

"Yes to both," Haig answered before Aislin could. She gritted her teeth and stared straight ahead.

"I'll see it done at once!"

"Sir," she called before the man could rush off. "I'll take a bath in the room now, thank you. But the dinner would taste much better downstairs among your patrons. Please have it served there. My companion is starving. For food as well as company."

The innkeeper took her meaning and bowed. "Of course, of course." He snapped his fingers and three of the wenches came to them immediately, smiling with their brightly-rouged lips and clamping down on any part of Haig they could reach to pull him away with them.

Haig sent her a murderous glare, to which she responded with a sweet smile as she accepted the room key from the innkeeper. "Enjoy your evening." Twirling her skirt around, she made a quick exit up the staircase to the room she didn't expect to be sharing with him. He'd be too busy with the wenches to—

A hand gripped her upper arm, yanked her around until her back met the hard surface of the wall. Disoriented, she stared into Haig's furious face. "Nice try, sweetheart, but you won't be getting off so easily."

"I don't know what you're talking about." She fought hard to keep her voice steady, but just standing so close to him made her heart thrash wildly. "I did you a favor." Gods-dammit, why did he have to affect her this way?

"You thought I would follow those overpainted whores like a starved dog to a feast and forget all about you. I gotta tell you, I don't know which part of that insults me more: the part where you tried to pretend you're no better than a tavern prostitute, or the part where you thought I'd let you."

His blue eyes gleamed with endless hunger—for her. He stared at her lips, slowly licking his own, and it was all Aislin could do to keep from pulling him into her. Desperate to regain her footing, she shook her head. "Haig, this is completely—"

He leaned into her, that starved-wolf stare boring straight into her soul. "It's like this, sweetheart." He fisted her skirt, pulled it up until he gripped the curve of her bare ass. Lifting her against the wall, he pressed himself between her legs, and Aislin wrapped them around him in automatic reaction. "I've developed an insatiable itch for this little pussy of yours." She gasped as his fingers skimmed across her opening. "I love the way you cream for me; I could eat you up for days." His eyelids lowered to half-mast, and he jarred her up a bit higher before letting her slide down—right onto his cock. "I've had a taste of what it feels like to be inside you, and I didn't want to leave."

Aislin bit her lip to hold back a moan as he slowly impaled her on his length to the hilt. And he watched her the entire time, breathing hard, unsteady. "And this…" He groaned, pulled back and thrust up, making her claw at his shoulders. She was so close already and, damn him, he knew it. "The way you grip me so tight, as if you never want me to stop."

"Haig," she gasped, curling her legs tighter around him.

"You want me just as much as I want you. Admit it, Aislin. Tell me, right now."

"Yes, *yes!*"

He rewarded her with a few hard pumps of his hips that set her off like fireworks. And he watched her come, kissed her gently as if in praise before he took his own pleasure, leaving them both gasping, leaning boneless against the wall's support.

"Every time you shut me out," he finally said, "it just makes me want to get deeper under your skin." He pulled out of her, set her carefully on her feet and let her skirt fall back into place. "I want you more than I've ever wanted anything before in my life. I want your hair curled around my fist, I want your scent on my skin. I want to fuck you until neither of us can walk, so you can never run away from me again."

"Haig, don't—"

He gripped her face in both hands, forced her to meet his gaze, kissed her hard until she melted into him. "And you can lie to yourself as much as you want, sweetheart, but I know you want me just as much. I see it in your eyes. You can't hide it from me. I'm too attuned to it by now."

"It was one night," she retorted, fisting her hands in her skirts. Damn him for saying all of this! She wasn't some naïve young ingénue about to fall for his pretty lies. But gods, how she wanted to… And what did that say about her?

Haig gave her that maddening half-smile again. "You don't even believe that yourself," he whispered. "Enjoy your bath."

Aislin watched him walk away, wondering how she'd ever let herself fall so hard, so fast.

CHAPTER 9

Never before had Haig looked at a woman and felt his skin crawl. He did now, watching one of the inn's wenches inch her skirt up her pale leg. A few days ago, he would have appreciated the come-on. He'd have enjoyed the show as she revealed her plump thigh and let the shoulder of her blouse drop so far he could see the top crest of her areola. He'd have pulled her onto his lap and bounced her up and down until her breasts spilled out completely and then he'd have gone to town on them until she melted in his arms.

Looking at her now, Haig felt nothing but disgust. Pale skin smothered with powder, unnecessarily red cheeks, garish rouge, bright yellow wig that hadn't been brushed in days… She looked like what she was: trash. So far removed from the reserved, vital beauty upstairs, they were almost a different species.

Haig took another swig of his ale and glared at the staircase where Aislin still hadn't appeared. How bloody long did it take to bathe? Even if the maid had to bring hot water up there in buckets, Aislin still should have been done and down here ten minutes ago.

Mug empty, Haig signaled the waitress for another, and endured the ostentatious sashay, the hip cock, and the lean-in to present her bosoms as she poured. She smelled rancid, like stale sourdough bread and alcohol. Haig waved her away, ignoring her pout.

Instead of leaving, the wench flashed brownish teeth stained with rouge and asked, "What brings you to our fine village, handsome?"

"Just passing through."

She hummed. "Perhaps you ought to stay awhile. See the sights. Sample our delicacies."

Seriously, was Aislin going to freeze him out again? He'd thought he'd made it clear he wouldn't be tolerating that nonsense. Maybe he should go up there…

The wench took a strawberry from the bowl and bit into it. "Our fruits are as sweet as honey. Won't you give them a try?" She all but shoved the rest of the strawberry into his mouth.

Haig brushed her hand aside and sat up with a sudden sharp inhale of realization.

Oh no… It couldn't be. *Oh, bloody fucking shite!*

He was brooding. *He* was *brooding*. Over a woman! "Dammit." How the hell had he let it come to this?

"Don't like this one? How about something else?" The wench took a crescent of orange, bit off a half and offered him the other.

No, this could not be happening! Where was his signature charm, his unwavering good mood and easy laughter?

It was one night, she'd said.

Bloody right, it'd been one night! He'd had thousands just like it, and would have thousands more before his heart gave out, quite possibly on another night like that. Made no difference in the grand scheme of things. Had it been great? Without a doubt. Excellent. Mind-boggling.

So what if every other version of him in every alternate reality out there seemed to be head over heels for her? That still didn't mean anything to *this* version. He still had free will, damn it; he could choose not to behave like a milksop. Aislin Crane was nothing special. Just another set of legs with a notch in between.

Is that why you're brooding now?

Haig shoved to his feet. He had to put a stop to this right now; take a walk, get some fresh air. Jump into the river and stay underwater until his balls froze off. That should put his head on straight.

He was almost by the door when the back of his neck prickled with awareness. Slowly, he turned around, looked up. And there she was, standing at the top of the staircase in that sexy feminine dress, one hand on the banister, the other pressed against her thigh. She'd tied her hair back at her nape like a girl fresh out of the schoolroom. Haig wanted to devour her in two bites.

Aislin descended a few steps, and he found himself coming forward. She descended a few more as he reached the foot of the staircase, with her a couple steps above. They stopped there, locked in some silent tableau: Haig looking up at her, hardly breathing, and Aislin watching him back, her eyes unsure, hesitant.

He didn't feel himself reach out, but in the next moment, her hand was in his and he was pulling her closer to tuck her arm into the crook of his and escorting her to the main room. Someone struck up a bawdy tavern song, and the tables all cleared as if by magic, the wenches pulling their men to dance.

In the midst of that din and noise, Haig and Aislin were smothered in silence. He pulled out a chair, intending to seat her, and somehow ended up in it himself, with Aislin sitting across his lap. She smelled like soap and woman, a fragrance more enticing than the most expensive perfume.

A bowl of stew appeared on the table before them, along with a bread basket. Haig took an oval of bread, tore off a piece, and offered it to Aislin. To his surprise, she took it, her lips closing around his fingers in a delicate kiss. It felt right. Familiar. Aislin wasn't just another set of legs anymore; she fit him, inside and out, and holding her like this, Haig realized that no matter where they went, in this world or any other, he'd spend the rest of his life wanting her just like this. And every night he spent mired in dreams of them in different realities, reliving memories of another life, that feeling of rightness became stronger.

They stared at each other, drifting closer…closer…

"Innkeeper! Your best fare for the king of thieves!"

Haig blinked hard, shook the ringing from his ears and looked across the inn to the entrance where a band of dandies had just entered. Four of them, all dressed in flashy purple capes, their black leather boots polished to a shine, and dapper white plumes stuck into each of their hats.

"Bollocks," Aislin muttered and tried to scramble off his lap.

Just to be contrary, Haig tightened his arm around her to keep her in place.

"Let go!"

"No."

She cast a wild look at the dandies, then back at him. "*Please.*"

Frowning, he released her.

The innkeeper rushed out from the back kitchen, two jugs of ale in each hand. He gaped at the dandies, then swept a deep bow. "Milords, what a pleasant surprise!" He almost spilled the ale as he gesticulated. "Please come in, come in!" Falling all over himself, he banished drunkards from the table next to Haig's, brushed it off with his apron, and invited the dandies to sit. "Martha! Bring the good wine! King Rolph and his merry company have come to call!"

Haig raised an eyebrow at Aislin who hunched down on his other side, hiding her flushed cheeks. "Friends of yours?"

"Play us a ditty, friend," one of the dandies demanded. Haig assumed this was Rolph. He wore thick, golden rings on every other gloved finger and a bunch of white lace at his throat. Swishing his purple cape over one shoulder, he revealed a thin rapier sheathed at his hip and a pistol stuck down the waist of his pants. Haig had to assume it was ornamental; weapons didn't work in the Elderwood.

The musicians struck up a tune, the wenches abandoned their partners to sidle up to the new group, and within moments, the innkeeper was back with a wine cask and two older women trailing behind him, bearing massive trays of food.

The dandies dug in with their gloved hands, while Rolph sat back with a chalice of wine and flipped a gold coin back and forth across his knuckles. He looked over the scene as a true king who took snobbish pleasure over the goings-on of the lower classes. Haig disliked him instantly. Rolph reminded him of the quintessential playground brat who could always get what he wanted simply by screaming long enough.

As if he felt himself the focus of Haig's attention, Rolph turned and their gazes clashed in silent challenge. Haig knew the man expected him to look away first and he took savage pleasure in denying him. But then Rolph frowned. "Aislin?"

On his other side, Aislin cursed softly, causing Haig to raise an eyebrow at her. "You kiss your mother with that mouth?"

"Aislin, I can't believe it's you!" In two jangling strides, Rolph had crossed the distance and caught Aislin up from behind, lifting her out of her seat and off her feet. Haig just barely restrained himself from breaking both of his arms. And legs. And maybe his head.

"Your Majesty," Aislin grated, prying at his hands.

Rolph released her as Haig slowly pushed to his feet, reminding himself that this had nothing to do with him. But when Aislin faced Rolph and he took hold of her nape and slapped that mustached mouth over hers, it was all Haig could do not to kill him.

Aislin knocked his hand away, shoved him off her, and somehow managed to draw his rapier in the process, leveling the tip at his throat. "Now Rolph, I thought we had an understanding."

He laughed in delight. "Oh, Aislin, I missed you." Holding his hands up in mock surrender he inclined his head. "Cry peace with me, beautiful, and join me for dinner. It's been too long. We have much to catch up on."

"Maybe another time," Haig cut in. "It's been a long day and we're exhausted."

As if noticing him for the first time, Rolph gave Haig a speculative once-over. "Who's your friend, dearling? He doesn't seem to play well with others."

Aislin lowered the rapier but didn't give it back. "Haig Cavanaugh, this is Rolph Saint Clair."

Rolph grinned. "You always were stingy with details. But I won't let you get away with it tonight, dearling." His taunting voice made Haig's skin crawl and, judging by Aislin's barely suppressed shudder, she felt the same. Haig mentally calculated the odds of taking the dandy down without causing damage and getting himself and Aislin banished for the night. Not good. He wouldn't risk it—unless Rolph put his hands on her again and gave him no other choice.

Aislin smiled, more a snarl than anything resembling a pleasant expression. "Haig is a fellow tracker. We're on a mission for Queen Snow."

"And…?"

"And"—she sighed—"Rolph is…*was* my—"

"Fiancé," Rolph finished. "We have quite a history, the Huntress and I. A lifetime ago, we were childhood sweethearts. Madly in love, weren't we, dearling? Our families didn't approve, but we were determined to run away and get married. We planned it perfectly for a night when my parents attended a royal ball and her father was sent to carry out a grave duty for Queen Zorana. I had my satchel packed, a pouch of coins tied to my belt, a golden ring in my pocket, and I set out for the Kissing Bridge where we were supposed to meet. Only…" He waited for Aislin to finish the tale. When she didn't he smiled somewhat coldly and said, "Only my beloved Aislin never showed up."

A sign of her good sense. Though he had to question her taste if she'd ever allowed a guy like Rolph anywhere near her. But Haig supposed everyone made mistakes in their youth. Not him, of course, but everyone else.

Without looking away from Rolph, she said to Haig, "That was the night my father took Snow White into the Elderwood. The same night I found out that on top of sleeping with my best friend, the boy I loved had schemed with her to drug the princess and make it easier for her to be dispatched."

Rolph shrugged easily. "She meant nothing to me." He didn't clarify whether he was speaking about Aislin's friend or Snow White.

"Juliet told me the same," Aislin confirmed. "That's what made it so easy to leave you waiting."

"I see," Haig murmured. And he was really beginning to.

CHAPTER 10

Aislin studiously avoided Haig's gaze, doing her best to remain pleasant. Not easy to do when Rolph looked at her with the same self-assurance he'd had as a teen, now ratcheted up several more levels, making her skin crawl. *Keep it together. He won't do anything while we're in the main room.*

Maybe not. But as soon as they left, Rolph would do what Rolph always did best: act like the whole world and everyone in it belonged to him. She'd have to warn Haig. They'd have to leave before Rolph decided to reminisce about the physical part of their relationship. Aislin just stifled a shudder.

"Shall we sit?" Rolph invited, but it wasn't a suggestion.

"Thank you for the gracious invitation," she replied, white-knuckling the hilt of his rapier even as she held it out to him. "But as Haig said, we're both exhausted. Maybe next time."

"Dearling, you wouldn't be planning to disappear in the middle of the night again, would you?" He took the weapon, curling his hand around hers so she couldn't pull away.

An unpleasant zing of sensation shot up her arm, making her hair want to stand on end. She gritted her teeth against yanking her hand free, something he'd consider a grave insult, and endured his touch for a second longer. She even managed a tight smile. "Not at all. In fact, we'd be happy to meet you back here tomorrow morning for breakfast. Wouldn't we, Haig?"

The glare Haig shot her spoke more than words ever could. "Up to you, sweetheart."

Great. Now they'd have a lovely pissing contest. Just what she needed. She unclenched her fingers to pull free of Rolph's hold, but as the last contact broke, the zinging sensation intensified. She frowned, rubbing the tips of her fingers with her thumb. This was more than just disgust. Something was…

"Well? What say you, lovely lady? A drink, a dance, perhaps more?"

"All right, that's it—"

"Yes," she said before Haig could say something that would get them both killed. "Yes to a meal and a drink. You're on your own with the rest."

Rolph smiled in triumph. "Excellent! Innkeeper, you heard her."

"I hear and obey," the old man retorted with a distinct lack of enthusiasm, retreating back to the kitchen for more food and drink.

Haig glared daggers at Aislin the whole three seconds it took them to be seated. Aislin ignored him, partly because his reaction didn't deserve a response, but mostly because she'd just identified what that odd feeling was, and she needed a minute to process it.

Touching Rolph had felt the same as reading ley lines. He was a clue. Either he knew where their target was hiding, or he was somehow involved in hiding him. Either way, they couldn't afford to leave him in the dust. The self-proclaimed king of thieves could be their best chance of completing the mission.

Now the only question was whether she'd be able to endure his presence long enough to see it done.

By the time their food had been brought out, Aislin had removed Rolph's hand from her thigh three times. By the time they'd finished eating, she'd shifted away from him twice, only to be pulled back against his side. By his third toast to her continued good health—accompanied as always by a shameless leer down her dress—she had to kick Haig to keep him in his seat. No way would she give him the satisfaction of indulging in physical violence. If anyone would kill

Rolph, it'd be Aislin.

The platters were eventually cleared to make room for more ale and wine. The musicians were instructed to play, and half of Rolph's company got up to accost the wenches. The other half was too drunk to stand upright. Rolph, however, remained wholly unaffected. He'd always been a master at holding his liquor. After rebuffing his invitation to dance and enduring his lecture on prudishness, Aislin had had enough. She peeled his hand from her waist, removed herself to sit across from him and tucked her feet under her chair, just to be safe.

A minute later, Haig jumped in his seat next to her. "Watch those feet, loverboy."

Rolph laughed. "My apologies. But can you blame me? Aislin has the most beautiful feet I have ever laid eyes on. Who wouldn't want to have them in his lap?"

At Haig's questioning look, Aislin shrugged.

Another leer, a grossly exaggerated air kiss, and Rolph dismissed her to focus on Haig. "So tell me, my friend, what brings you to these parts with the Huntress at your side."

"Just passing through."

"Indeed? On your way where?"

"Somewhere else."

Rolph smiled, the way he always had as a teen when someone had thrown a gauntlet at his feet. It made her nervous enough that she pressed her knee hard into Haig's in silent warning. They could not afford to start trouble. "Fabulous place, Somewhere Else. I've heard a lot about it. Tell me more."

Haig remained unfazed. "I'm a much better listener than a talker. And I heard you referred to as the King of Thieves. Is that right?"

Rolph nodded in humble acknowledgment. "Many do call me such, yes. But I aspire to nothing more than a peaceful life in the country. A little cottage, a plot of land"—he looked to Aislin—"a pretty wife... "

"A lot's changed since we parted ways, then," she retorted. "Last I remember, you wanted nothing less than to take over the world. A small cottage is a far cry from the collection of castles and palaces you were going to acquire by fair means or foul."

Yes, that was the ticket. Keep him talking, keep him distracted. If she could just focus hard enough, she might be able to find the link that tied him to their target. People were rarely reliable for navigation—they were too changeable, their moods and desires never the same from one moment to the next. But if Aislin could channel the queen's will through Rolph...

Rolph waved that aside. "Yes, well, clearly I succeeded. But it hasn't brought me the satisfaction I'd hoped for. It took me years to realize that no amount of riches would do that for me."

She picked up a faint sense of duty. She looked deep into his eyes, tried to somehow see into him. Energy flared around him in loops and swirls, tracing his every will and ambition, but one thread stretched in a straight line outward, faint and weak, as if worn away by time until little was left of its urgency.

"Well, that's a shame," Haig chimed in. "Seems all the ads for re-fined magic stock options have been lying to me for years!"

Rolph never looked away from Aislin. "Take my word for it, friend. Mountains of riches are a cold comfort when you go to sleep alone every night."

East. They needed to ride east. But how far? Aislin leaned forward a little more, pushed harder to gauge the distance. A day's ride, two at most. She sensed mist, water spraying out from a waterfall. A cottage tucked into a hill nearby.

"Maybe you should try a mattress instead."

That surprised Rolph out of his stare to look back at Haig, and he burst out laughing. "Try a mattress—that's a good one!"

"Well, it's really getting late. We should retire." Haig stood, dragging Aislin up with him. As soon as he touched her, her concentration broke and she lost the link completely. She stumbled, momentarily disoriented, and Haig steadied her against his side. "That last glass of wine was probably not a good idea. Let me help you. Gentlemen, good night."

Before she could protest, he dragged her upstairs, with Rolph and his suddenly sober and alert men watching them every step of the way.

Haig didn't trust himself to speak as they separated in their shared room, each to their own corner to get ready for bed. They only had the one bed to share, but for once, Haig didn't feel anywhere near in the mood for sex. The thought that Aislin had allowed such a creep to bed her was more than he could bear.

He checked their gear, locked the door, propped a chair against it, and opened the window wide. The night air was crisp after yesterday's storm, but summer was in high swing and the humidity was already rising, promising days of relentless heat before it broke again.

Aislin got into bed fully dressed, except for her boots, then snuffed out the light on her side.

Just to be contrary, Haig got in with her, keeping to his side, lying flat on his back with arms crossed over his chest so he wouldn't be tempted to reach for her. He expected Aislin to protest, but she didn't say a word. Haig listened to her breathe for a while, closed his eyes, and kept closing them every time they snapped open again. Too wired to sleep. He wanted to do something. Go for a hard ride, run around the village, punch someone's lights out—*something*.

"I can't believe you were going to marry him." The words burst out of him with enough force to jerk him up into a sitting position.

Curled on her side facing away from him, Aislin sighed. "I wasn't going to marry him."

"Obviously, you changed your mind in the nick of time. Well done there! But the fact that you would even *consider* it—"

"I didn't."

He scowled at her. "Yeah, sure."

She rolled over to face him, managing to imbue the simple action with enough exasperation to raise Haig's hackles. "*Maybe* I thought about it for half a second, but that was it. I knew about Rolph and Juliet long before he ever proposed. I knew about all of his girls. It wasn't like he bothered to be discreet."

"And you stayed with him, anyway?"

"I was sixteen," she muttered. "My exact thoughts on the matter were, 'But he still likes me best.' And then he proved it by proposing to me. But I still wasn't going to do it unless he proved to me he could stay faithful, so when I came home that night I told my father. I didn't care what Rolph did on his end, I wasn't going to keep secrets from my Da. And I definitely wasn't about to leave without saying something first. Da heard me out calmly, then bade me to sit and showed me a missive from the queen. She'd issued a royal order for him to remove Snow White from the castle and kill her, and she wanted the princess' heart as proof.

"The missive also said that he would have help from a castle maid, who would drug the princess to make her more compliant. The maid was Juliet, and I knew she could never have done it without help of her own. I also knew—and my father did as well—that there was only one person whom she'd ask for help; who could and *would* have provided that help."

"Rolph," Haig guessed.

Aislin nodded.

He laid down on his side to face her. "So what happened?"

She smiled sadly. "We fought. Da wanted to trick the queen by bringing her a doe's heart instead of Snow's. I thought he was completely mad. Zorana would have seen through it in an instant. I wanted him to run away—I even would have gone with him. We could have taken Snow White and disappeared.

"He said he'd never do that to me; that Zorana would never stop chasing us. Snow White was too important, and anyone who helped her would face the queen's wrath. Then he told me I had a duty to the true heir to the throne: to make certain those who wished her harm could never touch her. He didn't say it in so many words, but I knew what he wanted me to do. And he made me swear to do it, no matter what happened to him.

"The next day, he was supposed to take Snow White. I looked for Juliet, but couldn't find her anywhere. The castle cook told me her room was empty; she'd panicked and run away in the night without completing the task Zorana had given her. I knew that wouldn't absolve my father from his duty, which meant he'd either need help, or he'd have to lie to the princess." Her voice got softer the longer she spoke, as if the secrets of her past could still hurt her.

"So what did you do?"

Aislin swallowed hard. "I went to the princess myself and told her my father had invited her to his cottage near the Elderwood to see a family of rabbits he'd found. She did so love her animals. She also trusted us both; we'd never given her reason not to, so as soon as she finished her noon meal, she scampered off to the woods all on her own.

"And when the sun went down, I took my crossbow and went to the kissing bridge." She pulled her knees up tighter, squeezed her eyes shut. "I had him in my sights. A clean shot through the eye. He would have fallen into the river and gotten washed away silently before anyone noticed a thing. One shot, and my duty would have been done."

"You didn't take it." Clearly, since Rolph was still alive.

She shook her head. "I stood there for ten minutes with the crossbow to my cheek, just watching him pace back and forth. I had my finger on the trigger the entire time and I couldn't pull it to save my life. My arm got so tired it started shaking and I had to lower the crossbow, but I stayed there, watching him wait for me." Probably thinking the entire time that the boy she'd been sent to kill was waiting for her so they could get married. Haig couldn't imagine what that must have done to her. "Then, well past midnight, he must have realized I wasn't going to come. He hung his head for a minute and then he left. I trailed him off the bridge and into the city until he disappeared and then I broke down and cried. For hours."

Haig crooned, reaching out to rub her shoulder and back. "You were just a kid."

She scoffed. "Yeah. I was just a kid. You know the funniest thing about it all? My father still did what he had to, and he paid for it with his life. And Rolph still ran away with a girl that night. It just wasn't me. Da, Rolph, Juliet—I lost everyone I ever cared about in one day. And all because Snow White was fairest of them all."

CHAPTER 11

Even with the windows open wide and the night breeze ruffling her hair, Aislin couldn't sleep. Her brain was wide awake, jumping at every strange noise. She kept still so she wouldn't disturb Haig, but though he gave a convincing impression of sleep, she sensed he was just as awake.

Their conversation had come to an awkward stop earlier with Haig giving her a look as if he was on the verge of saying something before he blew out the oil lamp on his side and closed his eyes instead. Aislin didn't know what to make of that. Did he consider her weak now after her confession?

Well after midnight, the main room downstairs grew quiet, the last guests retiring for the night. Aislin tensed, watching light and shadows play across the gap under her door.

She wasn't disappointed.

Moments after all the lights went out, a pair of boots thudded softly across the hallway. No light, just the ominous sound of creaking floorboards stopping in front of her door. The handle squeaked as it was pulled down inch by inch until it encountered resistance.

Aislin pushed her blanket off to get up, only to feel Haig's hand on her elbow. He stretched lazily, then somehow stood from the creaky old bed without making a sound, padded to the door, and leaned his back against the wall, arms crossed over his chest.

The lock clacked open, the door pushed in, stopped by the chair Haig had propped against it. It closed and then pushed open again, hard enough to scoot the chair an inch farther.

"Lose your way, friend?" Haig asked.

Out in the hallway, Rolph chuckled. "I must have knocked on the wrong door. My apologies."

"That's a dangerous habit to have. You keep knocking on the wrong doors and one day one of them will open." He said it with such casual menace, Aislin felt a chill run up her spine.

"My mother gave me a similar warning whenever I stuck my fingers into jam jars," Rolph replied. "Ah well, some lessons just aren't meant to be learned."

Haig hummed in answer.

"Good night, then."

The door closed and locked, and moments later, Rolph's retreating footsteps faded into silence.

"Get some sleep," Haig said. "Come sunrise, I want to be hauling ass out of here."

"We can't."

He paused halfway back to the bed. "And naturally you have a good reason to think so."

"Rolph knows our target. He's connected to it somehow."

"And I care, why?"

She winced. "Because he may be our only chance of finding it."

Haig took a deep breath as if grasping for patience.

"I didn't want to worry you, but the trail in ley lines is weakening the deeper we go into the Elderwood. I may not get another accurate read the next time. Even Rolph's connection is faded. If we let him get too far, I could lose the trail completely."

He scoffed. "Figures. So what's your plan? And before you suggest it, we are *not* telling him or anyone else about the mission."

"Of course not! I'm not an idiot. We just ride out with Rolph tomorrow. As long as we're going in the same general direction, I'll have a trail to follow. When we hit a crossroads, we'll simply go our own way and let him go his. Hopefully, by that time, we'll be close enough not to need him anymore."

"Just like that."

"Yes, just like that."

"You may wanna rethink that 'I'm not an idiot' part."

She sat straight up. "Excuse me?"

"If you think Rolph will just let you go off again after you choose to ride with him, you *are* an idiot. A naïve idiot at that." Gone was the gentle confidant from before, replaced by a crass, arrogant, condescending jackass. The quicksilver change left Aislin reeling.

How quickly she'd let herself forget this was all a game to him. A few orgasms and her higher thought function switched off. For a second there, while she'd been pouring out her soul to him, she'd actually thought his concern was genuine. Gods, she *was* an idiot! "If you have a better idea, I'd love to hear it." Her voice was unsteady, her body shaking with pent-up anger—at herself as much as at him. "No? Then how about you shut your damn mouth and let me do my job?" Lying on her side, she clutched the blanket up to her neck and closed her eyes.

Haig was quiet for a while, still standing at the door. "Your job is to read magical trails: desire, intent." He spoke in a soft murmur so his voice wouldn't carry. "Whose desire are you reading when you touch Rolph? The queen's, or yours?"

She refused to dignify that with an answer.

Haig sighed and stretched out on the floor. "Seems to me like you're trying to fix your past with him somehow. Want to enlighten me as to which part? Just so I know."

Aislin gritted her teeth to keep from snapping back at him.

"If you want to kill him, you'll need backup against his merry men. I could help you if you asked nicely."

She put a pillow over her head.

"On the other hand, if you expect to pick up where you two left off, things might get a little awkward, since I'm not going anywhere. Think Rolph can handle a little competition?"

He made it sound as if she were some prize for men to fight over. After working so hard all of her life to escape the stigma of Zorana's reign, to make something of herself, to be worthy of respect, such casual mockery coming from Haig stung hard enough to make her wince. Aislin pressed down on her ear to drown him out, but it didn't work. His deep, almost rumbling voice permeated through her bones. Her body hummed like a tuning fork at the sound, even as her mind rebelled at the words he said.

"You're better than this, Huntress."

"Are you trying to convince me, or yourself?" she hissed, hurling her pillow at the indistinct shadow of his form on the floor. That he didn't trust her word was bad enough, but that he thought she would deliberately sabotage the mission to rekindle some old fling—with *Rolph* of all people!—was more than she could take. "Whose intent are *you* focusing on, Haig? My *desire* is to see this mission done. What's yours?"

"You," he replied, putting the pillow under his head.

No hesitation, no overblown declarations, just a single word spoken with quiet finality. And Aislin's heart gave an extra hard thump. She waited for him to say more, to laugh it off or put on a show the way he did with almost everything, but he remained quiet, and for the life of her she couldn't think of anything to say in response.

Both of them were up and ready by the time the sun had cleared the horizon, but at Aislin's insistence they stayed in until the main room filled with noise. When Rolph and his company made a loud entrance at breakfast, sounding their cue to emerge, Haig took Aislin by the hand and led her from the room. She didn't pull away, which was the only reason why he was able to keep a rein on his temper and not shove her against the wall again in the stairway.

That's what pissed him off the most. She was behaving like a juvenile, lovesick idiot. This whole ridiculous plan of hers was bound to get them both killed, and he felt like just as big of an idiot for even considering going along with it. And none of that had any effect whatsoever on how much he still wanted her. It was all her fault. He should have gone out for a wench or two after Rolph had crawled back under his rock last night. But he hadn't. Because he didn't want any wenches; he wanted Aislin.

Which made it all her fault.

And if Rolph turned on them and jeopardized the mission, it'd be her fault, too.

Keeping as civil a face as he could form, he seated her at a small window table across the room from Rolph the Bastard.

"Friends!" Rolph grinned wide, left his company and pulled up an extra chair to Haig and Aislin's table. The innkeeper rushed up to place a breakfast platter in front of him before he'd even asked Haig or Aislin their order.

"Aislin, dearling, you look ravishing this morn."

She did, as much as Haig hated to admit it. She'd dressed in her leathers again, but left her hair loose with just a couple of thin braids at each temple to keep it out of her face. With her mouth firm and her eyes sparking angrily every time their gazes met, she looked like a wild, sexy savage. She'd put her signature ice queen mask back on; hadn't said more than two sentences to him since his declaration last night—which, what the hell was that about? *She asks, "What's your desire?" and you say, "You."* Idiot.

And the worst part was she hadn't said she wanted him back.

"I trust you slept well?"

"Like a log," Aislin replied with a smile. "And you?"

I sit corrected. This was the worst part, the way she suddenly turned her adorably artless charm on some other guy. Haig narrowed his eyes at her. Two nights ago, she'd been wrapped around him like a demanding little octopus and now he might as well not exist.

Rolph waved her question away. "You know me. Sleep is a waste of perfectly good sex time. A shame you couldn't join me."

Ugh! Who said shit like that? Even at his worst, when he'd been out of his head with fever from infected war wounds, Haig had dropped better lines than that. Of course, he'd dropped them to Declan, thinking the Ravenskin healer was a buxom elf with somewhat mannish hands, but that was completely beside the point.

Aislin chuckled. "Maybe next time." Her tone was suggestive, but she couldn't meet Rolph's gaze. She was tense, visibly uncomfortable, but she never faltered in her forward press. If this was how she hoped to get a ride-along invite from her new BFF, gods help them both.

Rolph's eyes lit with interest that was a little too calculated for Haig's peace of mind. "Then maybe you should join us. We ride out this morning." *Chump.*

"Oh? Where to?"

It didn't escape Haig that he was in no way part of the exchange, and it pissed him off enough that he pulled Rolph's platter over and dug in without asking, just to get a reaction. It all tasted like sawdust.

"Gull Cove," Rolph said, ignoring Haig. "A little holding of mine on the eastern cliffs. Nothing but sea and rocks."

"Oh, I do love the sea." She looked at Haig, acknowledging his presence for the first time since the Bastard had joined them. "Haig, what do you say?" Her smile was a little too stiff to be genuine, and her posture, even leaning toward Rolph, was rigid, as if she was forcing herself into that position. For all of her talents, Aislin was a horrible actress.

Rolph, however, behaved as if everything was as it should be. Either he didn't notice the subtle signs of her distress, or he didn't care. Haig didn't know which option was worse.

Haig made a face and reached across Rolph for his tankard of beer. "It's awfully far out of our way."

"What's life without little detours, eh?" Rolph said to Aislin, as if she was the one who'd spoken. "Let me show you my home, dearling." Could he possibly have come up with a lamer nickname?

"I don't know," Haig replied, forcing himself back into the conversation.

Aislin bit her lip, immediately drawing Rolph's hungry gaze. The guy looked like he would swipe the table clean and fuck her right then and there. Haig wanted to rip off his head. "I think we can fit it in. We're going east, anyway." She reached for Haig's hand as he was bringing a forkful of scrambled eggs to his mouth. "Please, Haig? We can take the long way 'round, can't we? Please?"

He pretended to consider it, then sighed. "Fine. But if we miss the deadline, *you* explain to the queen."

Rolph threw his hands up. "Excellent! We'll wait for you by the stables." He sent Aislin a wink and a kiss. "I'll see you soon, my love." He took his sweet time getting to his feet, making sure to pause for effect so Aislin could get an up close look at the cockstand tenting his pants before he returned to his gang.

If they managed to make it until noon without Haig murdering someone, he'd call it a good day.

CHAPTER 12

Aislin's face hurt from fake-smiling all day. That's what she got for putting her ridiculous plan into action. Rolph had been only too happy to take her and Haig along, and the moment they'd ridden out from the inn, he'd devoted all of his energies to seduction. Well, his version of it, anyway, which amounted to his recounting their sex life in great detail to remind her how much she'd enjoyed it.

If she heard the words "succulent dewy quim" come out of his mouth one more time, she'd shoot him, mission or no mission.

By the time they'd stopped to make camp, she'd gone through all stages of embarrassment, disgust, anger, acceptance, and back to disgust so many times she couldn't dredge up enough energy for any more emotions.

Happily, Haig seemed to have plenty for both of them. And he wasn't shy about making them known. Aislin had to admit the man had a ruthless sense of humor. "Stand back, Saint Clair. I'm going to start a fire and I don't want you to burn down the whole Elderwood."

"Of course, we wouldn't want that. Come here, dearling, we must keep a safe distance from the flames." He reached for her and hissed as if burned, but kept tugging on her arm until he got her flat against him. "My, you are burning hot today, aren't you?"

Aislin gagged, looking to Haig for help, but all he did was raise an eyebrow as if to say, *This was your idea.* Traitor. "I should go hunt down something for dinner."

Rolph let her escape, but not before one last dig: "As long as you're dessert."

She'd never been so glad to leave the light of a campfire behind. Creeping through the forest, she listened for any rustle of nocturnal animals. She was on edge, distracted. This entire situation was turning out to be far more involved than she'd expected. She'd thought to at least have Haig's support along the way, a buffer against Rolph's advances, but the bastard had left her hanging. So much for, "I'm not going anywhere." Fat lot of good that did her if he wouldn't do anything, either!

"Aislin, my love, where *aaare yoouuuu*?"

Aislin froze. Rolph wouldn't dare come after her like this!

"I know you're close, I can feel it. Speak to me, dearling, say my name."

Suddenly a hard arm snaked around her, a hand pressing against her mouth as someone dragged her down behind a massive fallen tree. "It's me," Haig whispered at her ear, and Aislin rolled her eyes, tapping his hand over her mouth to get it off her. Of course it was him. No one else would dare sneak up on her like that, let alone succeed. The man they called Wraith lived up to his reputation when he set his mind to it.

He complied, but the arm around her middle stayed put.

"My beautiful Huntress loves to play games, I know," Rolph called softly, stomping across the dried foliage and scaring off all game. "But I'll catch you, dearling, like I always used to do." He passed only a handful of feet by them and never saw a thing.

Even so, Aislin didn't unclench until he was a fair distance off, still calling for her like some wayward dog.

"For the record, your ex is a dick."

She clawed out of Haig's hold and twisted around to face him. "Oh, and you're so much better?"

"Hey, this was your idea," he hissed. "If you recall, I wanted to leave the fucker in the dust!"

"Yeah, and you would have left the mission in the dust, too, but I guess that's all the same to you, right? Who cares what the queen wants, or what I want, as long as you get off. After that, it's to each her own!"

"What the hell are you talking about?"

"You! Don't even pretend this has anything to do with Rolph. You're just pissed that you can't get any while he's around."

She could have sworn his eyes flickered in the darkness. "Is that a dare?"

"What?"

"It sure sounded like one. Makes me want to take you up on it."

She scoffed, even as her heartbeat picked up a notch. "You're being ridiculous." Even more ridiculous was how eagerly her body responded to the sensual threat.

"Am I? Let's see." At the base of the fallen tree, where the roots shot out in gnarled tangles, the trunk had just enough curve to arch her back when Haig crowded her against it.

"Stop it," she whispered, even as she stepped her feet apart to make room for him. "Rolph's still out here. He'll hear us."

"Then you better be super extra quiet." With one leg snugly between hers, Haig pinned her in place and crushed his mouth to hers. Aislin should have pushed him away, but she couldn't. He kissed her almost desperately, his tongue sparring with hers, continuing the battle they couldn't have with words.

Aislin soaked it up like the first breath of fresh air she'd had all day. Her hands clutched the bark at her back at first, then curled into the waist of his pants. She bent her knees to grind herself against his thigh and Haig rewarded her by hitching his leg higher. His fingers dug into her hips, rocking her back and forth in a steady rhythm and his mouth never left hers, stealing air from her lungs until she grew lightheaded.

When he finally broke away to catch his breath, Aislin was so hot she wanted to claw out of her constrictive clothes. Soft mewling sounds slipped from her throat. Haig shushed her, trailing his mouth over her throat to a sensitive spot just below her ear. He knew it drove her wild, and he exploited it without mercy, kissing, licking, nipping, and all the while he rocked her against him, driving her closer and closer to the edge.

But it wasn't what she wanted. Hooking one leg over his hip, she raised up and pushed his lower body far enough to reach for the fastenings of his pants. He was so hard the seams strained and she struggled to undo the buttons, but as soon as she did, she reached for him, grasping the hard length of his cock in a tight fist.

Haig hissed against her throat, his body shuddering. When she gave it a long stroke, he froze, breathing hard, and caught her hand to stop her, visibly fighting for control.

"Told you, you couldn't do it," she taunted.

Haig reared back to stare at her and, though she couldn't see his face clearly, she felt him all but humming with masculine outrage.

Aislin hid a smile against his throat. "Oh well. You gave it your best shot." And she loosened her fingers to release him.

Haig's grip on her wrist tightened in response, he shoved her hand harder against his cock. "You asked for it," he growled, yanking at the laces of her pants.

She thrilled when they came loose enough to sink to her knees; stifled a squeak when Haig spun her around to face the tree. "Hurry," she panted, arching back toward him.

One hand snaked around her torso, gripping her breast in a firm hold, the other cupped her between her legs, hoisted her up to her toes. His fingers spread her wide, and he thrust into her as deep as he could go.

Aislin bit her lip to keep from crying out. She held on to the tree as he pulled all the way out in a slow glide, then thrust back in to the hilt. The third time he did it, he pinched her nipple through the leather of her bodice, eliciting a high-pitched squeak she couldn't bite back. He released her breast at once to cover her mouth. "*Shh…* You don't want the others to hear."

Her fingers dug into the bark for leverage. She tried to keep quiet, but the pleasure building inside her was too intense. And Haig kept stoking it higher, plunging into her hard and fast, stroking her clit at the same time. She pressed his hand harder against her mouth to muffle her moans.

Haig put his mouth to her pulse, lips moving against her skin with quiet words. Then he pinched her clit between his fingers and picked up speed, lighting a very short fuse to a spectacularly explosive climax. She clenched hard, her belly quivering, and only the hand at her mouth kept her shout from carrying to the camp while Haig pumped his hips a few more times, shuddering against her. His weight pinned her to the trunk, his body curled over her as if he couldn't keep upright anymore, and they stayed that way for a long time, until their breaths settled.

When her body cooled, the chill air nipping at her exposed skin, Haig pulled out and stepped away. Without a word, he rearranged his clothes, helped her put herself to rights. Then he raked his shaking hand through his hair, gave her a curt nod, and disappeared back into the darkness, leaving Aislin to muddle her way back to camp on her own.

Unsteady on her feet and not thinking clearly, she meandered through the darkness for a while, trying to make sense of what had just happened. She must have imagined it. Yeah, that was it. Her mind had played tricks on her in the night. The Elderwood was infamous for leading people astray. She'd thought herself immune to its effects by now, but maybe not. What other explanation could there be? No way had the infamous skirt chaser actually spoken those words against her throat.

Men like Haig didn't say, "I want to stay with you forever," especially not after three days. Not even in the throes of an orgasm.

CHAPTER 13

The company mood turned sour the next day. After his embarrassing strikeout the night before, Rolph looked at Aislin as if he wanted to throttle her. Haig might have enjoyed the show, if it weren't for the cold undercurrents going on between the King of Thieves and his men. All of them now had their capes pulled back over one shoulder, weapons in easy access. They spoke little, only amongst themselves, and always in hushed tones. Something was brewing. Haig didn't like it at all.

Even Aislin couldn't get through the ice. Rolph rode with his men, leaving her to follow with Haig, and every time she tried to catch up, they cut her off. When one of the merry men came too close to Emer, causing her to snort and prance back in agitation, Aislin took the hint and stopped trying. "I don't like this," she told Haig softly.

"Welcome to the club. What do you want to do about it?"

"I think it's about time we split off."

Haig snorted. "That'll go over well."

"Just slow down, let's give them a little distance. I can feel our trail veering off in a couple of miles. If they get far enough ahead, they might not even notice us splitting away down a different road."

He shrugged. Arguing would be pointless and it wasn't like he had a better plan. But just in case, he edged closer to Aislin. They slowed down, let the distance grow. Rolph's men definitely took notice. Someone whispered into Rolph's ear, and he checked over his shoulder with a quicksilver glance before facing forward again. Whatever he said in reply had his man nodding and moving off to give him space.

Two miles crawled by with Haig straining his eyes far ahead to see the fork. Except there wasn't one. Aislin had a permanent frown etched in her brow, her lips pressed together in a tight line. Rolph sure as fuck would notice them taking off into the woods. This was bad. All bad. "Slow down some more," he told her.

She did, her gaze glued to a spot farther ahead: a faint dent in the left edge of the road. A few yards past it, Rolph's company stopped and turned, waiting for them to catch up. "Something the matter?" he called back to them, no longer bothering with any pretense of civility. "We should pick up the pace. At this rate, it'll take us a week to reach Gull Cove."

"I changed my mind," Aislin said as they reached the dent. "I'm sorry, Rolph, but we can't continue on with you."

He looked her up and down. "Is that so?"

Aislin nodded. "I guess I didn't realize how far out of our way this would take us."

Rolph looked around, pausing at the dent a moment. "Strange place to stop."

"You're the one who stopped here," Haig said.

"We're getting too far behind schedule," Aislin told him firmly. "We can't risk missing the deadline. Royal orders."

Rolph smiled crookedly. "Royal orders. Yes, I remember. You're on a mission for Snow the Usurper. She didn't happen to send you after my charge, did she?"

As one, his merry men drew their swords and surrounded them.

Fuck. Haig pivoted Romper around to get a good look at their positions. "Oh, come on! Girl passes you over for a better man and you kill them both?"

Rolph ignored him, focusing hard on Aislin. "That boy did nothing but have the misfortune of being born to the wrong mother."

"Funny, I remember thinking the same thing about Snow White when Zorana tried to have her killed," Haig shot back. He couldn't look at Aislin. She was staring at him and he could feel her accusations spearing through him like her crossbow bolts. He knew what she was thinking, too, but with five men surrounding them with deadly intentions, he didn't have time to explain. *Dammit, I should have explained!*

"Would you like to know how close you got before you die? Yes, I think I'll tell you. Five miles down that overgrown little forest trail is a tiny little cottage huddled beside a waterfall glen. And in it lives a fifteen-year-old boy who's never stepped foot beyond the Elderwood. He knows nothing about the outside world, and he has no clue about his heritage, besides a hand-painted miniature of his mother and an old promise that one day she will come for him. Now, what kind of queen would send assassins after someone like that?"

"Haig," Aislin said, her voice small, broken, and he couldn't not look at her. The betrayal in her eyes almost knocked him from his horse. She clutched her reins hard enough to make Emer fidget. "Is this true?" Tears welled, but she stubbornly blinked them back.

Haig didn't know how to answer. To tell the truth would mean revealing a secret he'd kept his entire life, one that would make him a pariah and a target in all of Valefort. And if Rolph and his men survived to spread the word that Snow White had sent them after an ignorant boy living in seclusion, it'd be the end of her benevolent rule. *Think of something. Say something!*

He couldn't.

Aislin took his silence as confirmation. Her face shuttered as she pulled her hunting knife out of her boot. "Let's get on with this."

Rolph smiled cruelly and raised a hand. His men pushed in closer, waiting for the signal to attack.

"So I ask m'self, Wot's a flock of pretty gels in capes doin' 'round the 'untress and the Wraith?"

Haig gaped at the fat, bearded man strolling out of the woods.

"Don' seem sportin'-like, five 'gainst two. An' I tell m'self. If I lets 'em get snuffed, I'll never get m'knife back."

"Troll, have you been following us?"

"'Course I 'ave! Bloody 'untress wit the bloody Wraith traipsin' 'round my woods, bloody right I 'ave!"

"One chance, Troll," Rolph said. "Leave. Now. Raise a hand against any of my men and you'll be as dead as these two."

Troll grinned at Haig. "Remains to be seen." He whistled a shrill call, and all of a sudden the little stretch of dirt road filled with dirty men armed with knives and short swords.

Rolph rolled his eyes. "Kill them all."

Haig shoved Aislin out of her saddle a split second before the blade of a sword cut down. It sheared a hank off her hair, but at least it hadn't cut her through from shoulder to hip. Using his own momentum, he tumbled to the ground right after her. The horses spooked, stomping around in the fray. He risked their hooves to crawl over to Aislin and shield her as best as he could. She was unconscious and for a moment, holding her in his arms, Haig couldn't think past the panic that she might be dead. Turning her over gently, he found a gash on her temple, but her pulse was steady and she was breathing. *Thank the gods…*

Dragging her into the ditch for more cover, he looked over the battle raging around them. Rolph's men were too busy fighting the ruffians to notice them. Bedraggled they might be, but Troll had trained them well. They were smart, darting in to cut at the horses and running off before they got slashed or stomped. All of Rolph's men were now on the ground, defending against three or four each and having a hell of a time scoring a single hit.

Rolph, meanwhile, kept his horse moving as he searched the ground for Haig and Aislin. They'd underestimated him. It galled Haig that he'd gone against his instincts. He'd known Rolph would be trouble the moment Aislin had told him about the bastard's alliance with Zorana, but he'd let himself get distracted by Rolph's play for the Huntress—an obvious cover. How the fuck had he missed it?

I let her get to me. Even as he thought it, he knew it was a lie. He hadn't let her do anything. He'd *demanded* it. Haig had wanted her from the minute she'd walked into Snow's boardroom, and he'd been determined to make her want him just as much.

"Aislin, wake up. Open your eyes."

Rolph spotted them. He sneered, clutching his sword so hard his entire arm quivered.

"Aislin!" Haig shook her, eliciting a pained moan.

Rolph spurred his horse forward straight at them. No time to run. Haig did the only thing he could: pulled Aislin beneath him, covered her head, and prayed to the gods she'd live through this.

Aislin's brain felt far too big for her skull. Her ears thundered with noise, the ground at her back vibrated. She heard an indistinct voice calling for her; tried to answer, but her mouth wouldn't work properly. *What happened?* The last thing she remembered was…

Aislin sucked in a breath, opened her eyes in time to see the stricken look on Haig's face just before he rolled over her, smothering her beneath him. A horse screamed, and she cringed, clutching at Haig. *Too close!* It'd fall right on them!

And it did. The great hulking beast dropped onto its side right on top of them, slamming down hard enough to make Aislin's lungs reverberate with the impact, cutting off her shout. Haig grunted over her. Their bodies jarred left and right, back and forth, as the animal struggled to its hooves and took off down the road.

Aislin blinked. "Haig? Haig, talk to me! *Haig!*"

He groaned, raising his head enough to look down at her. "You okay?" he rasped. A horse had just fallen on his back and he was asking if she was okay.

She snatched him back down to her, overcome with so much relief that for a moment she couldn't breathe. He murmured something indistinct in her ear, pulled her arms away so he could get up. They were in a ditch. As Haig pulled her up to sit, inspecting her head wound, she saw the furrow in the ground was just deep enough to hug them. It had sheltered them from the horse's impact. That made twice now Haig had saved her life in less than a half-hour.

Registering the silence around them, Aislin looked out at the road. Rolph's men were on the ground, all dead. Troll stood over Rolph himself as his ruffians tied him up. Emer and Romper were securely in hand and a couple of men were trying to calm the horses that hadn't run away. The battle was won.

Troll came over to them. "I'll 'ave that knife of mine now."

Haig handed it over hilt first. "You have my thanks, Troll."

"Aye, well. Anything for the 'untress." He winked at her. "Told you, me men are *profes'nals*. What'll ye want done wit that one?"

Haig looked at her askance.

"I'll take care of it," she said with difficulty. She'd never taken a human life before, but she had to do this. For her father.

"Are you sure?"

Aislin nodded. "Help me up."

Haig pulled her to her feet, caught her against him when she swayed. "You don't have to do this."

"Yes, I do." She pushed out of his hold and retrieved her crossbow from Emer's saddle as Troll's men dragged Rolph to his feet to face her. She didn't look at any of them; didn't respond when Haig said her name. If Aislin acknowledged them, she'd never be able to do this. And she had to do this. Once and for all. "Rolph Saint Clair," she said, putting a bolt to her crossbow and sighting down its length, "you are charged with conspiracy to commit treason and regicide against the true queen of Valefort. A sentence which carries with it the penalty of death. How do you plead?"

Rolph spat blood at her feet. Troll's men had worked him over without mercy. His face was beaten to a pulp and he couldn't stand unaided. "Fuck Snow White! The true queen of Valefort was Zorana, and her son—"

Aislin's bolt pierced his throat before he could finish the sentence. He gurgled, eyes bulging as blood bubbled from his lips. Aislin pulled the string back once more, put another bolt to it, aimed, and shot him through the eye. His head snapped back with the force of impact and stayed there as his body went slack, held up by Troll's men. They laid him out on the road and dusted off their hands.

Aislin turned away, fighting tears. *It was right*, she told herself. *It was justice long overdue.* She busied herself putting her weapon back in its place while Haig and the men talked. Their words passed through her without sticking. She'd just killed a man who would have murdered an innocent girl for the queen's asking.

And she'd agreed to track and help murder a boy just as innocent for the same reason.

The knowledge made her stomach roil. Turning away from Emer, she fell to her hands and knees and cast up the little she'd eaten that day. She felt Haig approach, but didn't have the strength to move. He brushed her hair away, rubbed soothing circles over her back in solicitous concern. His touch now made her cold. "We can't do it," she said, wiping her face. "We can't kill a little boy."

"Sweetheart, no one said anything about killing him."

Aislin made herself look him in the eye. She saw no hint of deception in them, but then again, she never had before, either. "What?"

Haig shook his head, glancing around at the men pulling shined boots off the corpses. "Not here." He helped her to her feet again, keeping hold of her waist to ascertain her balance. "Can you ride on your own?"

She felt shaky, with her knees on the verge of buckling and her hands cold and numb, but she nodded. The alternative was riding with him, and Aislin didn't think she could handle so much prolonged contact.

He nodded and said to the others, "Gentlemen, you have our thanks for your assistance. You've plenty of loot there already, but allow me to add a little token of my appreciation." He withdrew a pouch from his saddlebag, hefted its weight in his hand to jangle the coins inside. With practiced precision, he tossed the pouch to Troll. "Do we part as friends?"

Troll opened the pouch and grinned. "A pleasure to run into ye again, friends. May'ap our paths will cross in the future." He tipped an imaginary hat, whistled, and he and his men retreated back into the forest, taking the extra horses with them. The corpses they left laid out in the road as a warning to travelers. But they'd removed Aislin's bolts, leaving no evidence of who'd done the deed.

"Now what?" she asked numbly.

"Now we have a mission to complete."

CHAPTER 14

Just as Rolph had said, five miles down the overgrown forest trail the woods opened into a glen. A gentle waterfall poured down the side of the mountain into a creek big enough to hold fish. The surrounding meadow was covered with hip-high grass and bright yellow flowers stretching toward the sun. At the forest's edge, someone had built drying racks for meats and furs. Several game hens hung there by their legs, and a beaver pelt was stretched out to cure.

The squat little cottage might have been picturesque two decades ago, but had fallen into disrepair since then. The roof was haphazardly patched, the walls had holes between the logs. One window shutter looked torn off, the other hung on by a prayer, but someone had put a planter in the window and it was thick with blooms of every color.

Haig had known all along what they'd find at the end of this trip, and his gut still clenched at what he knew needed to be done. He couldn't imagine how Aislin had to be feeling. Rolph's execution had left her rattled. She hadn't said a word the entire ride here, lost in her own thoughts with a thousand mile stare. Now that they were here, she looked around listlessly, and it physically pained Haig to see her this way. "How's your head?"

"Fine," she replied. He didn't believe her. The gash on her temple had stopped bleeding, but it was swelling up, and her gaze wasn't quite focused. She could have a concussion. It didn't ease his mind any when she almost fell out of her saddle trying to dismount.

Haig was at her side in an instant, catching her against him. She rested her head against his for the briefest instant, as if holding it up was too much effort. Haig hugged her close. "Hold on to me, sweetheart. We're almost there."

"We can't kill him," she said again.

"I know. We won't."

"I'll stop you if you try."

The momentary flash of temper heartened him. "I'd expect nothing less. Come on, let's go inside."

No one around that Haig could see. He called out to make sure, but when no one answered, he led Aislin into the cottage. Its insides matched its outsides. The small room had a bed, a table and chair, and a large wooden chest for storage. That was it. Dried herbs hung from the exposed rafters, permeating the air with a mixture of scents. A black cat slept curled up by the fireplace where a small pot bubbled over a dying flame.

Haig sat Aislin by the table and added another log to the fire. Didn't know why he bothered; no one would be around long enough to eat the stuff, anyway, but something about that smoldering pile of coals was just too…depressing. He smoothed a hand over the cat's back while he was there, enduring its half-hearted hiss before it then settled back to sleep.

Spying a covered pitcher on the mantle, he took it down and sniffed at the contents. Water—perfect. He filled the chipped earthen cup with its handle broken clean off and brought it back to Aislin. "Drink this. It'll make you feel better."

She didn't look at him, nearly fumbled the cup when she reached for it, as if her depth perception was skewed, but she obediently took a couple of gulps before setting it down onto the table. Task completed, she went back to staring off into space with eyes turned bleak, all spark of vibrant life depleted.

Haig waited for her to say something. When she didn't, he sighed and sat on the edge of the worn, neatly-made bed. "It won't be long.

He'll come back eventually." Before sunset, at the latest.

"Why would she do this? Why ask this of us?"

"Snow White?"

Aislin nodded.

Haig sighed, so damn tired of cleaning up after the bitch Zorana's psychotic rule. "Do you remember what Valefort was like after her father died? The first thing Zorana did was levy a tax on raw magic and punish anyone who used it without permission. You couldn't see it much in Kesteran, but out here… Overnight, people who depended on raw couldn't afford it anymore. Crops withered, cattle died, women miscarried. A man had to choose between watching his family starve, and going to jail for ten years just to see them fed for a single night. And Zorana had eyes *everywhere*. She saw *everything*.

"She built herself up to almost god status, turned Valefort into her own, sadistic amusement park, trampled tens of thousands of poor people into the dust in the process. Valefort would have crumbled from the inside out if Snow White hadn't stood up to her.

"This boy is heir to that. It doesn't matter whether or not Zorana's evil had passed down to him. He's a male child born after his mother's marriage to the king, which makes him the legitimate heir to the throne. If anyone ever tried to put him on it, Valefort wouldn't see *him*, they'd see a male version of Zorana. Whether or not Snow White chose to challenge him, and regardless of his intentions for the kingdom, there'd be no preventing another war. And this time, I don't think Valefort could survive it."

"So the boy has to go."

"Yes."

"Even though he doesn't know anything about any of this."

"Rolph knew, which means others do, too. That's all that matters. As long as he's here, he's a threat."

Aislin looked at him, her eyes bleak. "What will you do with him?"

The door burst open, admitting a winded waif of a boy, his cheeks flushed red and his eyes bright blue. "I heard someone calling," he said, gasping for air. He looked like he'd run a mile to get back. "Have you come to take me home?"

Aislin stared at the boy in front of her, the spitting image of Zorana, and she understood why Haig was so determined to get rid of him. Just looking at him gave her a pang of irrational fear, as if the evil queen was looking out through his innocent eyes. If she had this powerful a reaction to him, what would others feel? Zorana might have been dead and gone, but her memory was still alive. It wouldn't take more than this boy walking into Kesteran to set the kingdom on its ear.

Which meant Haig was right.

Gods, she hated this.

"Hello," Haig said. "What's your name?"

"Haven't got one," the boy answered, staring at them expectantly. "Don't you know it? They said you would."

"Who did?" Aislin asked.

"The men who brought me here." He rushed to the wooden chest and rummaged through it, tossing out thick books and worn silk scarves until he pulled out a small, silver box inlaid with gemstones. The metal was aged to black in the seams, but the exposed surfaces had been lovingly polished to a shine. The boy brought it to the table and set it before them. "They gave me this and said it was a gift from my mother, that one day she would come back for me."

Haig said nothing, so Aislin carefully opened the box. Inside lay an old letter almost falling apart from being folded and refolded countless times. The regal script was faded from the page, unreadable in places, but Aislin had no doubt the boy knew it by heart, backwards and forwards, after so many years. She scanned it briefly, but saw nothing in it about kingdoms or thrones, just a message of love from a mother to her son, telling him they couldn't be together now, but that one day, when it was safe, she'd send for him. The tender words were so incongruous with what Aislin knew of Zorana she didn't know what to make of it.

Handing the piece of paper to Haig, she reached back into the box and pulled out a miniature. Her hand shook as she beheld Zorana's painted face. The evil queen been beyond beautiful, with her mane of golden hair elegantly arranged around her delicate, pale face. Her jewel-blue eyes stared dispassionately out into space, her lips were painted blood red.

"That's my mother," the boy said. "It's all I have of her."

Aislin managed a smile. "You look like her."

He beamed, puffing out his narrow chest. "Have you come to take me to her? Can I take Mouser with me? He won't cause trouble at all, I swear!" Before either of them could answer, he set about tossing the few things he owned onto a square of cloth on the bed to make a bundle. "I'll be ready in a snap. Don't go away!"

"Boy," Haig said with difficulty, "stop for a second and have a seat. I need to tell you something."

The boy stopped. With his back to them, he said, "It's bad, isn't it?"

Haig nodded, even though the boy couldn't see.

"You haven't come to take me home."

"No."

His young shoulders sagged. He turned and sat on the bed, head bowed. "Have you come to kill me, then?"

"No," Haig said again. "I came to give you a chance to live."

Aislin looked on as Haig sank to his haunches before the boy and coaxed him to look up. He didn't have a weapon in sight, but a man his size didn't need one against a teenager. Aislin tensed, reaching for her knife just in case.

"Your mother isn't coming for you. She… I'm sorry. She died."

The boy nodded. "I thought she might have. After the men stopped coming, I figured something must have happened."

Haig looked back at Aislin. She could guess what he was thinking. Rolph must have been charged with caring for this boy. When Zorana had died, the selfish prig must have figured no one would care if he left the boy to starve. Except, from the looks of things, Zorana's son thrived here, all alone in the Elderwood. Abandoned and isolated. Aislin's heart broke for him. He didn't deserve this.

"What if I told you I can make it better?" Haig's tone raised Aislin's hackles. "I could take you from here to someplace else. Somewhere with people who would love you and take care of you as if you were their own. Would you like that?"

"Haig…"

The boy stared at him for a moment with a gaze so direct Aislin shuddered, but Haig held steady. "Can I take Mouser with me?"

Haig nodded, then twisted around and held his hand out for the miniature. Frowning, Aislin handed it over. "Take this, too. And anything else you don't want to leave behind."

The boy kissed the miniature, then wrapped it and the letter in a silk scarf and put it in his bundle, leaving the ornate box behind. Haig gently picked up the sleeping cat, enduring the grumpy yowls as he placed him on the boy's lap. "Hold on to him."

Then he put his hands on the boy's shoulders and the air around them wavered like a mirage.

"Stop!" Aislin cried, rushing forward but his magic held her back.

"Don't move, Aislin. Don't touch him."

She tried anyway, and was repelled by an invisible force. "Haig, don't do this!"

He didn't respond. Boy and man stared at each other, insulated in a magical cocoon Aislin couldn't penetrate, no matter how hard she fought, or how loudly she screamed. Then something began to change. The boy started fading like a ghost before her eyes. Color leeched from his skin, his hair, even his clothes. He became transparent, then only his outline remained like a glass shell where a human being and his cat had sat.

A moment later, that shell disintegrated from the top down, melting away in a sparkle of magic, and within seconds, Zorana's son, his cat, and his bundle were all gone, and the magical force field shrank back into Haig.

"What have you done?" she whispered.

"What I said I would." Haig pushed to his feet, but didn't get very far. Ashen-faced, he sat hard on the bed, rubbing his brow with a shaking hand. "I don't kill people, Aislin. Well, I did, in the war, but that's not what my Gift does."

"Explain," she demanded. "Make this make sense!"

Haig sighed. "My magic alters reality. It erases things and people from this reality and transplants them somewhere else. Outside of this cottage, the boy who used to be Zorana's son no longer exists—he never did. Instead, somewhere out there, in another reality, a barren old couple has a son who will love them and take care of them for the rest of their lives. He'll grow up to be a good man, and he'll make a good life with some pretty village girl, and only he will ever know that once upon a time he had a different mother in a different world, who'd died before she could come back for him."

Aislin sat down hard. "So…he's alive?"

Haig nodded.

"And no one will have to kill him anymore?"

"Not unless he sleeps with the wrong man's wife."

"Why didn't you tell me about this?"

"Would you have believed me? And if you did, would you have ever trusted me again? With anything?"

No, she wouldn't have. "So we're finished now."

Haig looked at her, his face carefully blank. "Is that what you want?"

She wanted to get the hell away from here; to put some measure of distance between herself and this whole gods-damned mess of an assignment—including Haig. "The mission's over. We need to report back to the queen."

"She won't know what the hell you're talking about."

"Even so, I—"

"Aislin."

"No!" She shoved to her feet, swayed, and caught herself against the windowsill, knocking down the planter in the process. It shattered on the ground outside. "The mission is over. There's nothing more for us to discuss."

"Isn't there?"

Aislin made the mistake of looking back at him. His pale cheeks heated, his eyes blazed. The muscles in his jaw twitched angrily, but he sat utterly still, staring at her with so much yearning it made her heart ache. "Please, don't do this. We both know you're not in this for the long haul. How long before you get tired of me and leave? Or maybe you decide it's easier to just get rid of me like you did with the boy—"

"I couldn't."

"Because you just care about me so much?" She scoffed at that.

"Yes," he growled fiercely, his hands fisting. "And because even if I was stupid enough to try it, I could only send you to a reality where a version of me exists." His breath hitched. "And you're already there. In every single one of them. With me."

He sounded so earnest, Aislin wanted so badly to believe him. But she'd been swayed by a skirt chaser's pretty words before. "I can't." If she gave in, let herself trust him, and he broke her trust, it would kill her. She leaned her back against the wall. Gods, this hurt. "The longer I stay, the harder it'll be to watch you walk away."

Haig's eyes turned bleak. "You don't believe me."

Aislin shook her head. "I'm sorry."

"So last night, when I said I'll want you forever, meant nothing to you."

"It was just the sex talking."

"Right. It was just the sex." Why did he sound so bitter? She was giving him a clean out. Wasn't that a good thing? Haig Cavanaugh couldn't possibly want a clingy female trailing after him because he happened to spend a few nights with her and said a few silly words.

I want to stay with you forever.

Damn him for making this so difficult! Aislin took a deep breath to rally herself so she could manage a smile when she looked back at him. "Maybe our paths will cross again. I'd like that. But let's not pretend this is anything more than it is. We both know better."

He stared at her for a long time before giving her the slightest of nods. "As you wish."

CHAPTER 15

They decided to stay the night in the cottage to rest up for the ride back to the city. Both of them were a mess after all was said and done; Aislin still wasn't steady on her feet and Haig passed out cold the moment his head hit the pillow, thoroughly drained by his magic trick. But they both agreed that there'd be no harm and "no funny business" if they rode out together the next morning.

They fucking *agreed*.

So when Haig woke up to an empty cottage the next day, he was righteously pissed that Aislin would just leave him in the dust like that. And right on the heels of that anger came a sharp stab of fear. Anything could happen to her in the Elderwood—the entire place teemed with criminals, magical things, and wild animals, and Aislin was injured, coming off five days of hard riding, relentless fucking, and a shit-ton of emotional distress—she was in no condition to go off on her own.

How many damn times would he have to save her gorgeous ass before she bothered to look past his reputation and realized he could be trusted?

Haig wasn't exactly looking for a Happily Ever After here. Aislin was great in the sack, sure, but she was a royal pain in the ass the rest of the time. Haughty, opinionated, argumentative show-off with a heart of ice. If he were stupid enough to fall for her, he'd spend the rest of his life having shouting matches with her on a daily basis, followed by more of that awesome, sweaty, take-your-breath-away sex. And yeah, his dick stood up to salute that idea, but what the hell did it know? A life like that would be hell for him. And for Aislin.

Right.

So, she'd been right to put distance between them, and he was glad she hadn't taken his words to heart. Would he want her forever? Sure, in the sense of "I want to fuck you until neither of us can walk," but he'd had tons of women like that in the past. Couldn't exactly remember any off the top of his head, but that didn't mean anything.

He was Haig Cavanaugh, for fuck's sake! He was not a one-woman guy!

The only reason this whole thing pissed him off was because she'd just left him in the middle of the night without saying a word. What if he'd had a heart attack or something in the night? What if she got jumped by thieves and rapists on the way? They were partners, dammit, they were supposed to watch each other's backs. At least until the mission was complete—reported and off the books.

With that thought forefront in his mind, Haig saddled up in record time and set off to catch up with the ice queen bitch.

Except he never did.

Two days of a breakneck ride got him back to the Elderwood's border, without a single hint of Aislin's presence. She must have ridden without pause. And that meant she'd likely already reached Kesteran and reported to Snow.

Haig slowed as he approached the final tree line. She'd left him. He breathed in deeply, rubbed at his chest to relax the weird muscle cramp feeling around his lungs as he pulled Romper to a halt.

The trees gleamed with the faintest hint of magic. Rumor had it the Elderwood was a sentient being, steeped in raw magic, and people who entered it became altered in some inexplicable way. Haig had never given it much credence. Unless curvy nymphs were involved, he didn't pay attention to superstitious claptrap. Waste of time, anyway, since magic always did what it wanted to do, whether people realized it or not. In the end, magic was an engine of Destiny, and Destiny would always take its course.

But standing there in that moment, Haig could almost believe. He felt different; his insides didn't fit the way they'd used to. His gut was clenched for no reason at all, and his chest felt somehow hollow and constricted at the same time. Even the prospect of going back to Miss Kiki's Bawd House failed to summon his signature good cheer. Now it suddenly felt like a chore.

Haig nudged Romper forward, emerging from the Elderwood through a wall of static that made him shudder. Before him, the valley lay wide open. Kesteran glittered in the distance, a shining beacon of home, and it bothered the hell out of him that he rode toward it as if he had a gun to his back.

By the time he'd reached Miss Kiki's, he was exhausted and in no mood to talk. Still, he left Romper in the hostler's able hands and dragged his feet inside.

A chorus of eager female voices greeted him on sight. He waved in greeting, making a beeline for the empty armchair by the hearth and collapsed into it with a bone-weary sigh. A couple of the girls came to him immediately, crooning the day's specials, playing with his hair, tugging at the neck of his shirt. Their faces were nothing but a blur of indistinct features and bland smiles. Haig offered a half-hearted, "Thanks, loves, maybe later."

They left him with mewling pouts and pleas for him to come to them after hours. Haig was relieved when their colorful dresses retreated from his periphery. Staring into the hearth fire, he relaxed for a while, beginning to doze off when a deeper voice called out to him. "Haig?"

Roused from a half-sleep, Haig frowned. "Beau? What are you doing here?"

Beau rubbed the back of his neck self-consciously. "Queen's orders." He still wore the Rebel Court uniform from their audience with Snow White days ago. Only now, the cufflinks were gone, his shirt was open down to his navel and only half-tucked into his pants.

Haig's eyebrows shot up. "The queen ordered you to get laid? Oh, man, that's embarrassing. I'm sorry it had to come to this."

Beau turned bright red. "Will you shut up? That's not what this is about."

Maybe, but even a guy with Beau's iron will and unflappable self-control couldn't spend time among these women without getting a leg over one way or another. As evidenced by the fact that for the first time since Haig had known the young man, his hair was a bird's nest and he looked a complete, disheveled mess. "Should I congratulate you now or later?"

Beau didn't rise to the bait. "Is something wrong? You look like hell."

Haig rubbed his stubbled chin. He didn't doubt that for a minute. "Yeah, I'm fine. Mission accomplished. All's well that ends well and all that shit."

"Doesn't sound like it ended all that well. You're about a month's worth of hair growth away from Graeme status."

"Ouch, Beau. That was harsh." So he might have missed a bath or two, and hadn't shaved in a few days. But how bad could he have looked to warrant a comparison with the wolfman?

"I just mean you look like you've been through a battle. What happened?"

Haig waved the question away. "Got into a bit of trouble with the Huntsman's daughter."

"Oh?" That one sound brimmed with interest. Suddenly, Beau was sitting next to him, leaning forward as if he couldn't wait to hear the story. Which Haig wasn't about to recount.

"It's nothing," he said. "It's over. Back to life as usual."

"Right," Beau retorted. "So you won't be seeing the Huntress again?"

The simple question should have produced a simple answer from Haig. Instead, it bounced around in his head, demanding that he actually give it some thought. And when he did, Beau's talk about some big to-do at the castle turned into background noise, and it dawned on Haig that he wasn't anywhere near finished with the heartless Huntress bitch. "Beau," he said, pushing to his feet, "I'll see you later."

He pretended not to hear Beau shout, "You're welcome!" at his back as he raced out of the brothel.

Aislin made good time getting back to the city. She was tired, but relieved when she rode Emer into the castle stables and dismounted at last. Her ass sore, and her legs tingling from the endless ride, she took the long way around to her private suite of rooms to walk it off, then took a quick shower, changed her clothes, and returned to the grand hall. "Aislin Crane to see her Majesty," she said to the receptionist.

The woman dialed a number. "The Huntress to see her Majesty. Yes. No, she didn't have an appointment. I understand. Thank you." She hung up and smiled at Aislin. "Her Majesty will see you in the boardroom."

Aislin nodded thanks and followed the pointing finger.

The boardroom was empty, but the tables were scattered with files and half-drunk glasses of water. Snow White, dressed in another impeccable skirt suit with her shining black hair twisted into a thick coil at her nape, was seated at the far end, reading something on her laptop computer screen. When the herald announced Aislin, Queen Snow looked up and smiled, standing to welcome her. "Aislin, it's good to see you. Please, come in."

Aislin approached the tables and bowed respectfully. "I apologize for coming to you unannounced. This won't take long. I just thought you'd want to know right away that the mission is complete."

Snow's smile turned quizzical. "Mission?"

"Yes, your Majesty. The one you dispatched me on with Haig Cavanaugh."

A quicksilver frown creased the queen's brow before she nodded. "Ah, yes. A mission for Haig. And you are certain it was completed?"

"Absolutely, your Majesty. I was there to see it done."

The queen hummed in answer. "And how did it go?"

Aislin hesitated. "There were no loose ends, your Majesty."

"Yet you look troubled. Is everything all right, Aislin?"

She forced a smile. "Nothing that needs concern you, Majesty. It's only a personal matter." As soon as she made herself believe that Haig was gone for good, she'd get on with her life as before, and with time, that annoying pinch of regret over what might have been would fade. Nothing to it. Time healed all, as they said. Maybe once enough of it had passed, she'd stop wishing her bed wasn't empty in the night.

"I'm sure," was Snow's skeptical reply. After a pause, she added, "Your head looks like it could use some TLC."

You have no idea.

"I want you to see my physician before you return to your duties."

"As you command, Majesty."

"Off you go, then. And thank you again for everything."

Aislin bowed and took her leave.

The herald led her directly to the castle infirmary, but instead of the old, balding woman Aislin expected to find there, a massive Ravenskin greeted her at the door. Aislin steeled herself not to flinch when he speared her with a harsh, metallic silver stare. "The queen sent word to expect you," he said not unkindly, but his deep voice was so ominous, Aislin couldn't respond right away. She felt herself staring at him, but couldn't stop. "Please, do come in. I won't bite." Then he smiled, his bright white teeth gleaming against his raven-black skin and she wondered how she'd ever thought he looked menacing.

Aislin stepped into the exam room and sat on the table where the Ravenskin indicated.

"You're Aislin Crane," he said. "I knew your father. A good man."

"Yes," she said. "He really was."

"My name is Declan Rave, and I assure you, you have nothing to fear from me."

"What's your real name?" she asked, then clamped her mouth shut, mortified that she'd dare to bring it up. Ravenskins were considered cursed, a blight. Most were killed at birth. Those who survived were stripped of their names so their curse wouldn't pollute the family line.

The physician raised an eyebrow. "My mother's name was Jennings."

"It's nice to meet you, Declan Jennings," she replied to cover up her atrocious faux pas, but as she stared into those shimmering eyes, she realized she meant it. Smiling, she offered her hand, and after a curious moment, he shook it.

"Let's take a look at that gash, shall we? Are you hurt anywhere else?"

Aislin shook her head. "I don't know. Probably. It's been a trying few days."

He studied her face for a moment, then his expression softened. "Lie back and relax. This won't take long." When she did, he leaned over her and shone light into her eyes. He examined the injury on her head, then straightened and placed one hand on her abdomen and the other on her forehead.

"You're one of the Rebel Seven," she said.

"Yes," he answered shortly.

"I just returned from a mission with one of your colleagues, Haig Cavanaugh."

"So I've heard. Hold still, please."

The warmth of healing magic poured from his hands and settled over her entire body, soaking into her like sunshine, and within moments her head felt as good as new, her aches and pains were gone, and she'd even regained a bit of energy. It made her feel a little giddy, and before she'd had a chance to think about it, she heard herself ask, "What was he like during the war?"

"Haig?"

Aislin nodded, watching him.

Declan frowned, his face taking on a foreboding quality, but he wasn't looking at her. His gaze had turned inward as he remembered the past, and Aislin could tell he made an effort to give her a proper answer. "Fierce. He had a disturbing way of throwing himself into each task, despite how much he hated performing it. The queen's dog, they used to call him, because he always obeyed without question; did things no one else had the stomach for.

"I think that's why he spends his days in brothels now: to balance out the darkness with a bit of pleasure." His silver eyes flickered as he searched her gaze. "He gives a convincing impression of a right scoundrel, but that is the farthest thing from who he really is. He just knows that if people knew what he was capable of, they'd fear him. A man who balks at nothing makes for a dangerous enemy. But to those who earn his loyalty, he's just as fierce an ally."

"I'm sure."

"He'll do whatever it takes to get his way. If the goal is important enough, he'll give up the shirt off his back, his pride, even his life and soul, if need be."

"I believe you," she said with a frown.

The Ravenskin flashed a smile. "Do you?"

Did she, really? "Yes." If nothing else, Haig had proven his willingness to do whatever it took to serve Valefort and its queen. Matters of state naturally ranked high on the importance scale. One wench among many? Not so much.

With a thoughtful hum, the physician removed his hands and his magic, and allowed her to sit up. "Well, the good news is no serious damage was done. You're all set, and ready to resume daily activities as normal."

"What about…"

"Yes?"

Aislin blushed. "Any diseases I need to worry about? Or…um…" She touched her hand to her abdomen.

Seeming to catch her meaning, the physician tilted his head. "No, no diseases, or pregnancy. Would you like a charm to prevent it?"

There'd be no reason for it. Haig was gone and she wasn't likely to start having sex with someone else anytime soon. Still, she nodded. "Yes, please."

He produced a pendant from one of the many drawers lining the wall. Holding it in his fist, he let his magic flare for a moment, then handed the charm to her. "Wear that against your skin for as long as you don't want to get pregnant."

"That's it?" It was such a small thing, just a flat, metal disk with a symbol etched into it on both sides.

"That's the power of magic. But, I'm sorry to say, as grand as it is, it still can't heal a broken heart."

She flushed. Exactly how deep did his magic touch go? Could he read thoughts? Test souls? She'd heard of magical creatures with such powers, and Ravenskins were born of magic. It stood to reason…

Gods, what if he told Haig and all the other Rebels, and they laughed at the idea? Desperate to avoid that kind of humiliation,

Aislin forced a careless chuckle. "Oh, my heart's not broken, trust me. It was just a fling. Meant nothing." Of course, it hadn't—it had only been five days!

"If you say so," he replied, watching her closely.

Aislin took her leave and quickly returned to her rooms. She ought to get a few hours of sleep in a proper bed. Usually, after a trip to the Elderwood, she took a couple of days to recuperate before she set out to her normal duties again. Her team of woodsmen always took good care of the game in her absence—she had no reason to think otherwise now, so no reason to rush out.

Still, Aislin felt restless inside stone walls. Opening the window wide, she breathed in the aroma of fragrant flowers. A hundred different varieties bloomed in the royal gardens and they changed with the seasons.

Their scent had always been a source of comfort to her. Today, it felt cloying.

Aislin closed the window and laid down on her bed. Two minutes later, she was up again, pacing the spacious suite. Five minutes of that, and she was stuffing her feet into a fresh pair of boots and stomping back outside. She needed a walk to clear her head.

A footpath through the gardens led to a little plank bridge across a creek. The path then continued on through a sparse forest to the Huntsman's cottage at the edge of the Elderwood where her father had used to spend most of his time. Aislin hadn't stepped foot in it since the war. Too many painful memories.

They all came back to her as she walked the path now: her father taming a falcon with a gentle hand; carving out her first bow; showing her how to fletch the arrows. He'd raised her to take over his duties when the time came, and Aislin had never doubted she would; she'd been too good at it from the very beginning. She'd just never imagined it would happen so soon.

At the end of the path, the cottage stood exactly as she'd left it, with the shutters closed and the cages empty of rabbits. The shed was padlocked to keep all of her father's treasured tools safe. Every single one of his bows and knives was in there, even the ones that had chipped or broken with age. She walked up to the cottage door and pushed down on the handle to let herself in, bracing against the world of heartache she knew waited for her inside.

The musty smell of aged wood hit her nose and made her eyes sting. *I miss you, Father.*

Suddenly, a voice spoke from the shadows, making her jump. "So there I was, strolling along without a care in the world, when I came across this charming little cottage."

Aislin's heart skipped a beat. She gaped at the man who'd made himself at home, his booted feet propped up on the dusty table and his chair leaned back on two legs. "W-what—"

"I thought to myself, 'What a charming little place! I've been strolling for a while, I must be close to the Huntsman's lands now. Why, this could be his fabled cottage! And didn't someone mention that there was a family of rabbits living nearby?'" He dropped the chair onto all fours, and his feet thunked down onto the floor. "I love rabbits, you know. So I figured I'd look around a bit, see if I can't find them. But, alas, nary a single bushy tail to be seen. I looked, and looked—and I gotta tell ya, looking is hard work! I got tired pretty fast, so I figured I'd rest for a spell."

"How'd you get in here?"

"The door was unlocked."

"But—"

"Now, I know what you're going to say. You weren't supposed to see me ever again, we were finished, nothing more to discuss, blah, blah, blah. *But.* You did say our paths might cross again, and that you'd like it. You did say that, Huntress."

She nodded, still trying to process the fact that Haig Cavanaugh was standing in her father's cottage, talking to her as if there was something left to say.

He grinned, and it was like watching the sun peek out from behind cloud cover. "Well, I guess our paths just crossed a little sooner than either of us expected."

"Why?" If he expected her to fall for another one of his games, he'd be sorely disappointed.

Haig came to her, the bright smile giving way to an expression far more intense and serious than she'd ever seen on his face. He took her hands in his, looked into her eyes and said, "It's like this, sweetheart. I'm not ready to see this thing between us end, and I don't think you are, either." He paused for her to say something, and she should have, dammit, but her mind was completely blank, just basking in the feel of his thumbs rubbing back and forth across her wrists. Taking her silence as confirmation, he continued, "So I have a proposition for you. A bet, if you will."

Aislin scowled. "I am not agreeing to any more bets with you."

His eyes twinkled with mischief. "I think you'll like this one. Give me one month with you. Thirty days. That's all I ask. Let me show you I can do this relationship thing and make you happy."

What had Declan told her earlier? *He'll do whatever it takes if the goal is important enough.* Aislin looked deeper, past the twinkle in Haig's eyes and the irreverently raised eyebrow, to the sharp edge in his smile, the pulse beating out a rapid tattoo in his neck, and the rigid tension in his shoulders.

The carefree skirt chaser was nervous.

"If I do, you'll admit that you misjudged me and agree to be my girlfriend, with the possibility of raising that to wife at some future date."

Her jaw went slack. Had he just said he wanted to marry her?

"If I don't—and for the record, that is a big *if*—you'll tell me where I messed up and give me another month to fix it. With the certainty that I'll get it right this time, and after the sixty days you will admit that you misjudged me and agree to be my girlfriend, et cetera, et cetera." Her face must have betrayed a hint of weakening resistance because he dropped the jokes in a hurry to pounce on it. "I know you don't believe me, but I meant every word I said to you in the Elderwood. *I* didn't leave you, Aislin. *You* walked away from *me*. You never gave me a chance. That's all I'm asking from you: a chance."

Looking into those brilliant blue eyes, she believed him. He *had* told her the truth every step of the way, and somewhere in those five days they'd spent in the Elderwood, his words had changed from "I want you" to "I'll want you forever." Somehow, during that time, Aislin had come to want the same. Irrational as it was, it felt too real to ignore; she was heart-deep in trouble already. But could she trust him to really mean it? Aislin swallowed with difficulty. *Gods, I think I might.*

Of all the rumors and gossip floating around Kesteran about the consummate seducer Haig Cavanaugh, not one of them had ever involved any broken promises. Quite the opposite—he'd always seemed to go out of his way avoid commitment of any kind. The queen trusted him unequivocally. His brother-in-arms eagerly defended him.

And here stood the man himself, asking her for nothing more than a chance to prove himself.

Why not take the chance? She'd already put her heart out there for him to crush beneath his boot heel—why not risk it a little while longer to see if it might not actually work out between them? It'd be a huge gamble, but a chance at happiness with Haig might just be worth it. Because somewhere in the last five days, "happiness" had lost its appeal when it didn't included him.

"Look at it this way," Haig tried again when she still hadn't answered. "At best, you get to brag that you caught the uncatchable Haig Cavanaugh and your legend as the Huntress will live on forever! At worst, you get a new polishing rag for your collection."

Aislin bit the inside of her cheek to keep from laughing. *I can't believe I said that to him—in front of the queen, no less!* "Aye, well…fine."

Haig whooped and crushed her to him, slanting his mouth over hers as if he'd never stop. And suddenly,

Aislin's world felt right again.

ABOUT THE AUTHOR

ALIANNE DONNELLY was a wordsmith long before she became a reader. Driven by an insatiable curiosity about everything from history and mythology to science and philosophy, she grew into a fiction writer who hates coloring inside the genre lines. Her books all have elements of romance, with different series sorted under paranormal, science fiction, fantasy, and erotic. And then there's *Wolfen*…

Alianne lives in California, doing hard time in a corporate 9-5, while secretly scribbling away any chance she gets. She loves pizza, hiking, and avoiding small talk, and hopes to one day win the lottery jackpot.